THE VISCOUNT AND I

Forever Yours Series

STACY REID

THE VISCOUNT AND I

Edited by AuthorsDesigns

Cover design and formatting by AuthorsDesigns

Dusean, always and forever.

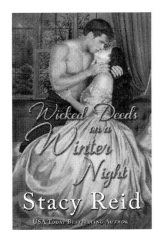

Happy reading!
Stacy Reid

that I look for when reading romance and deserving of a 5-star review. "—*Isha C., Hopeless Romantic*

"Wicked in His Arms—Once again Stacy Reid has left me spellbound by her beautifully spun story of romance between two wildly different people."—*Meghan L., LadywithaQuill.com*

"Wicked in His Arms—I truly adored this story and while it's very hard to quantify, this book has the hallmarks of the great historical romance novels I have read!"—*KiltsandSwords.com*

"One for the ladies...**Sins of a Duke** is nothing short of a romance lover's blessing!"—*WTF Are You Reading*

"THE ROYAL CONQUEST is raw, gritty and powerful, and yet, quite unexpectedly, it is also charming and endearing."—*The Romance Reviews*

OTHER BOOKS BY STACY

Series Boxsets

Forever Yours Series Bundle (Book 1-3)

Forever Yours Series Bundle (Book 4-6)

Forever Yours Series Bundle (Book 7-9)

The Amagarians: Book 1-3

Sinful Wallflowers series

My Darling Duke

Her Wicked Marquess

Forever Yours series

The Marquess and I

The Duke and I

The Viscount and I

Misadventures with the Duke

When the Earl was Wicked

A Prince of my Own

Sophia and the Duke

The Sins of Viscount Worsley

An Unconventional Affair

Mischief and Mistletoe

A Rogue in the Making

The Kincaids

Taming Elijah

Tempting Bethany

Lawless: Noah Kincaid

Rebellious Desires series

Duchess by Day, Mistress by Night

The Earl in my Bed

Wedded by Scandal Series

Accidentally Compromising the Duke

Wicked in His Arms

How to Marry a Marquess

When the Earl Met His Match

Scandalous House of Calydon Series

The Duke's Shotgun Wedding

The Irresistible Miss Peppiwell

Sins of a Duke

The Royal Conquest

CHAPTER 1

Hanover Square, London

I'm to be married, finally.

A fierce joy sparkled inside Lady Frances Elizabeth Dashwood, Fanny to her close friends and family. Her dear mamma had long despaired this day would ever come, considering Fanny had been the cause of a most dreadful scandal several years past. A disgrace that had sent her papa to his grave, or so her mother, the dowager countess often lamented, even though Papa had died four months after the unfortunate incident.

It had taken years, three to be precise before Fanny had been tentatively enfolded back into the bosom of society. How glorious it had been this season to finally attend balls, musicales, and ride through Hyde Park once more, without ladies lifting their fans and cutting her, without speculative whispers, and the dreadful conversations that abruptly ended whenever she approached. Of course, being courted by Harry Basil, the Marquess of Trent had been the feather needed to set her cap upright.

And today they were tying the knot at St. George's, Hanover Square. Determined to look ravishing, she'd worn a fashionable dress of the palest pink silk, which accentuated her curvy figure to its best advantage. She'd caught her blonde hair up in the most elegant of chignons with becoming wisps framing her face, and a coronet of flowers woven between the strands. Today was to be a most splendid day, and Fanny ensured she appeared the most elegant and perfect bride.

The ceremony was to start in fifteen minutes. Her carriage had already driven around the square a number of times because her mother was so eager that her daughter had landed a gentleman of such esteem, but it would not do for her to be waiting in the church on him. Her mother was glowing with pleasure at the prospective match. Fanny thought it absurd but had agreed to remain in the carriage until the marquess reached the altar. She had done so to settle her mother's nerves. Fanny had never been one to display emotions of any sorts in public, and she had needed a few moments to herself.

Her carriage paused at the grand frontage of St. George's and a footman jumped down to confirm whether the Marquess had arrived. Apparently, his carriage had delivered him on her previous circuit of the square. Her step was let down, and she was helped down by the footman. She smiled at him nervously as she straightened her shoulders to climb the steps to the entrance. It was hard not to be intimidated by the imposing façade with its six Doric pillars and Grecian triangular frieze. Her mother in the second carriage would organize the bridesmaids and follow her up. Her brother Colin, the current Earl of Banberry should be waiting in the porch for her and then they would proceed up the central aisle on the red carpet to the altar.

She opened the church door and entered, taking a left turn down an isolated corridor. She faltered as she spied a couple ahead. The man appeared familiar. Something terrible and fearful gripped Fanny's heart and a cold knot twisted through her stomach. For precious seconds she was unable to comprehend the sight. The man she was to marry was locked in the most passionate of embraces with a lady Fanny recognized as Miss Miranda Shelby. Fanny only had cause to know Miss Shelby for she had been the unfortunate recipient of vulgar rumors which claimed Lord Trent had offered this woman *carte blanche*. She had asked her brother for clarification, and he had refused to mortify her sensibilities. Against her brother's advice, she had asked her betrothed about Miss Shelby, and the marquess had re-assured Fanny, his friendship with Miss Shelby was in the past.

The hot sting of tears burned her eyes. The loving way he placed her palm on his cheek and the tender smile on his lips belied his assurances and promises given only last week. A crushing weight settled against her chest, and an alarming sound of pain slipped from her. The two lovers were too enthralled with their moment, to notice Fanny hovering on the threshold.

"Oh, my darling, I cannot bear that you are to be married. How I despair I will lose you," Miss Shelby cried, crushing the marquess's hand to her chest. Her bosom heaved over her low-cut gown, her golden ringlets bobbed with her agitation, and Fanny suspected the lady's light blue eyes glistened with tears.

"You will never lose me," Lord Trent vowed fervently. "As soon as possible my sweeting, I will order Lady Fanny to the country, and she will remain there until I say otherwise. Nothing will sway my love for you…" Then he lowered his hand to the gentle protrusion under her gown. "I will be with you every step of the way when our babe comes into this world."

They kissed fiercely, their ardor for each other mortifying, and an arrow of envy and sorrow darted through Fanny's heart. She desperately wanted to flee, but her limbs would not obey her. She was frozen, the pain hammering through her terribly. Lord Trent had professed to love her, had showered her with acceptable gifts, and had even stolen a few kisses, a liberty she had allowed for she had been so sure she loved him in return.

All evidence showed he was ardently caught in the throes of passion with Miss Miranda Shelby. The few indelicate rumors Fanny had heard, could no longer be denied. She turned away, a harsh sob tearing from her throat, and hurried down the hallway. Tears blurred her vision and hating the notion the marquess might exit and see her fleeing, she clutched the skirts of her dress and ran.

"Fanny?"

With a gasp she halted, pressing trembling fingers to her lips. "Mamma…" How she wished she could fling herself into her mother's arms.

"My dear girl, you are fleeing as if the devil is on your heel. It is not seemly." The countess glanced behind Fanny, her elegant brows puckered in a severe frown.

She allowed her mother to tug her toward a hidden alcove near the entrance that would lead her to the altar.

"What is amiss, Fanny?"

She desperately tried to swallow past the pain in her throat. "Lord Trent…"

"Yes?"

A flush traveled along her body. "I saw him just now, clasped in a most improper embrace with Miss Shelby."

Her mother considered her as if she had never seen her before. "And this is what has you so out of sorts?"

Confusion rushed through Fanny. "Mamma, they…they were declaring passionate love for each other, and kissing most salaciously," she whispered, beyond mortified to be revealing such intimacy to her mother.

"Pish. Today is a most auspicious day, and the

only thing that is important is in a few minutes you will be a marchioness. Lady Trent. The likes of Miranda Shelby should never upset you. She is too low to be given any prominence in our thoughts. Now let's set you to rights, for the ceremony is to start."

Fanny grappled for a precious moment to perceive her meaning. "Mamma, I cannot marry a man who has no regard for me, and on the day we are to marry he is professing his devotion——"

"Nonsense," her mother said sharply, her dark green eyes flashing with ire and determination. "Men will always flatter their vanity and have their mistresses. It's the way of the world, and we do not let it bother us. As ladies, there are far more pressing matters to occupy our attention."

Fanny recoiled. "You are speaking in jest, of course! The fidelity and the honor of the man I marry cannot be suspect. Mamma——"

Her mother gripped her chin in a painful clasp, shocking Fanny into silence.

"You will listen to me, Fanny Elizabeth Dashwood. You were foolish enough to break your betrothal to Viscount Aldridge because it was revealed it was your fortune which attracted him. It took years for society to forgive your outrageous behavior. You are on the cusp of being a marchioness, and you will not ruin your chances and bring disgrace to this family again."

Disgrace.

She trembled at the reminder of how intolerably unforgiving society had been when she had rejected the viscount weeks after her initial acceptance of his proposal. She made no reply, for Fanny was a mess with the emotions rioting so forcefully inside.

"Gather your composure, we have a wedding to attend."

Then her brother appeared from inside the church, and she was hustled down the aisle on his arm so that he could give her away.

Several minutes later, Fanny stood at the altar of the cathedral, facing the marquess, who did not have the appearance of a man who had been passionately making love to another. He peered down at her with familiar tenderness. She had been so confident he loved her. Was she so naïve and desperate for a family she had allowed a libertine to deceive her? How could she have been so mistaken in his heart and character?

Colin stated that he was giving her away before taking his seat.

The bishop began the ceremony, and she bit the inside of her bottom lip to prevent the tears burning behind her eyes from spilling over.

"Dearly beloved, we are gathered together here in the sight of God, and in the face of this congregation, to join together this man and this woman in holy matrimony; which is an honorable estate…"

Please stop talking! It would not do to be fodder for gossip on her wedding day. Nor must she bring disgrace to her family. Lifting her chin, she squared her shoulders and met the gaze of the man she would pledge to love and obey for the rest of her life. He winked, a charming habit he had whenever he wanted to make her smile. But now she saw the emptiness and the lies for what it was. He did not love or esteem her, it had all been a cruel charade with a purpose she could not understand. The marquess did not desire her fortune, for society knew he commanded fifty thousand pounds a year. It *hadn't* been because she was an heiress.

Lord Trent had courted her so ardently with the sweetest of poems and flowers. All those long walks in the park, the picnics, and the dancing at balls. They had meant nothing to him for his plan was to send her to the country, while he resided in passionate bliss with the woman he loved. Fanny trembled, and Lord Trent frowned, concern darkening his eyes. *Liar*, she wanted to snarl, hating that she was reduced to this mess of pain and anxiety on a day she had been anticipating since her sixteenth birthday.

"Henry George Basil, Marquess of Trent, wilt thou have Lady Frances Elizabeth Dashwood to thy wedded wife, to live together after God's ordinance in the holy estate of matrimony? Wilt thou love her, comfort her, honor, and keep her in sickness and in health; and, forsaking all other, keep thee only unto her, so long as ye both shall live?

"I do."

It was becoming more difficult to breathe by the minute.

Fanny perceived she was poised on the cusp of the scandal of the season. She would make everyone forget the jubilation of their beloved Queen Victoria's coronation, and last week's disgrace of Sebastian Rutledge—the Iron King—in refusing to marry Miss Arabella Sutton, despite being caught in a compromising situation with the lady. No, Fanny's scandal would be like no other.

The slice of pain that went through her heart made her tremble. *I will lose everything I have been hoping for*. To marry this man after what she had witnessed…

"Lady Frances Elizabeth Dashwood, wilt thou have this man to thy wedded husband, to live together after God's ordinance in the holy estate of matrimony? Wilt thou obey him, and serve him, love, honor, and keep him in sickness and in health; and, forsaking all other, keep thee only unto him, so long as ye both shall live?"

A dreadful silence blanketed the church as the bishop waited for her affirmation. Why had she allowed herself to be persuaded to the altar? A murmur of voices penetrated her panicked thoughts, and her gaze snapped to the dozens of guests in attendance. Only one hundred or so people were present to witness the joining, but it felt as if all of society waited in judgment. If she did not commit now…if she truly walked away, she would be *ruined*, and nothing would render her respectable.

The knot in her throat was growing.

Her mother paled and gripped her brother's arm who seemed to observe something was wrong. Colin slowly stood, his hands clenching at his side, a warning flashing in his expression.

The bishop cleared his throat the action shaking his jowls.

"Lady Fanny, is all well?" Lord Trent asked, peering down at her.

"I saw you," she finally answered. Her throat felt thick, and there was a tightness across her chest that made it difficult to breathe. "I saw you…with your mistress." A woman who also waited in the pews. How did she dare stand watching the man she loved marrying another? Humiliation clawed through Fanny at the memory of how they had clung to each other only a few moments ago, and the whispered words of promises her fiancé had vowed.

The marquess stiffened, knowledge darkening his pale blue eyes. He reached for her gloved fingers, and to the onlooker, his clasp would have seemed gentle. But her fingers ached from the way he subtly twisted them. She tried to yank her fingers back, but there was no give in the marquess's grip.

Something awful must lurk within her, for she knew to walk away would be the ruination of all her dreams and the reputation she had struggled to reclaim. Fanny desperately wanted her own family. She was three and twenty and after the last fiasco three seasons ago when she had called off her engagement to Viscount Aldridge, the scandal had been terrible. The viscount had even threatened to sue her family for breach of promise, and her father had settled an unnamed sum on him. The scandal sheet had dubbed her the runaway heiress, and for the longest time, Fanny had thought society would never accept her back again.

But they had, and she had crept from the shell she had slipped under to protect herself from their vicious gossiping, and cruel scrutiny. If she did not marry the marquess now…everything she had wanted for so very long would disappear like ashes with the wind.

Lord Trent lowered his head. "You will confirm your vows now," he warned, twisting her fingers, grinding the knuckles against each other.

A low whimper escaped her, and her heart quaked. Another revelation flowed through her soul. Not only was he a libertine who planned to order her to the country and be wicked with his mistress, but he was also cruel. This was a man who would not hesitate to beat her if she should dare defy him. How could she have been so mistaken in his character?

"You will release me, or I shall scream."

He ignored her, and Fanny slapped him. His

expression of comical dismay filled her with satisfaction. Then she walked away unable to look into the faces of her guests, especially her dearest friends and close family. With every step she felt the awful weight of their shock and judgment. Eyes followed her, the whispers of shock accumulating and cresting in a swell through the church. The news would spread through society like wildfire, and her family might never forgive her. The scandal sheets would burn for weeks with this spectacle.

Unable to walk serenely down the aisle, she ran.

CHAPTER 2

"Have you heard?"

Sebastian Rutledge now Viscount Shaw danced lightly on his feet, avoiding the hammer like fists of his closest friend and business partner in a housing venture, Percy Taylor. They had been boxing now for almost an hour, and though Sebastian's muscles burned, and sweat dampened his hair and body, he was nowhere near ready to throw in the towel. "Are you attempting to distract me, because I am winning this bout?" he asked with a grin, slamming a right into his friend's side, his thinly wrapped knuckles meeting hardened slabs of muscle.

Percy had been obliged to offer himself up as a

sparring partner and had arrived at the crack at dawn at Sebastian's townhouse in Berkeley Square. Sebastian had been restless, eaten up with a sense of anger and despair that was quite unlike him. He was known for his calm, methodical approach to business and personal matters, and he prided himself on being practical. This release of energy was the best thing to divert his thoughts from the sense of loss eating through his soul. His friend had suggested he visited a bawdy house and released his frustrations in one or two willing female bodies, but Sebastian had been unable to confide he had been without a woman for over two years. Because of *her* —Lady Fanny Dashwood, a woman who didn't even notice his existence beyond the barest of polite social conversation. He was a damned fool.

"So, you really have no notion," Percy said, a taunting smile on his lips.

They circled each other now, both getting in another punch before Sebastian replied, "Notion of what?"

"Lady Fanny ran away from Lord Trent. They are not married."

And that was all Percy needed to say to knock the wind out of Sebastian. The man took advantage and clipped him on the chin, and he allowed himself to fall backward on the ground with a resounding thud. The ache of that didn't even penetrate, nor did the ringing in his head. *Lady Fanny wasn't married*. The reason for his tormented restlessness would not be slowly unwrapped tonight by another man and out of his reach forever. He was the worst sort of scoundrel to even feel for a minute the primal satisfaction that slammed into his gut.

"You knew she was marrying today." Percy stood above him, unwrapping the thin leather from his hands. "I thought *that* was the reason you wanted to spar so desperately. Good God man, when are you going to realize fine ladies like her ain't for the likes of us?"

Never. But he made no reply. "Are you certain she is unwed?"

Percy scowled. "If you had been out instead of holing up in your townhouse, you would have heard. The news is all over town. Lady Fanny slapped Trent's cheek and then ran away from the altar and into her carriage. From all accounts, the lady's action is ruinous. Rubbish if you ask me."

Sebastian went cold. *Ruined*. He did not want that for her, not when he had discreetly observed how being cut had hurt her. Sebastian had met her a few years ago at a dinner party to which her brother, Lord Banberry, had invited him. They were friends of sorts, for a while Sebastian was certain he commanded the respect of most of the fashionable lords because of his wealth and business shrewdness, though he did not belong to their elevated circles. The title of Viscount had been conferred upon him only two years past, just because the previous viscount, a cousin twice removed had been unlucky enough to die without an heir.

Society had been amused with Sebastian's lack of refinement to his embarrassment. It seemed a grave sin that he had not been born into wealth and power, and worse still his father at one point had been a butler before he had made his wealth through trade. The few times he had attended a society event, those who fancied themselves his better, had treated him with a thin veneer of courtesy, and he had been quite conscious he was not considered to truly belong to their society and probably would never be fully accepted.

The only worthwhile thing that had resulted from the few balls he'd attended was meeting Lady Fanny. At their first meeting, Sebastian had been struck by her prettiness and charming manners.

Several times he had bumbled in his speech around her, and he had been flummoxed that he could feel so witless from a smile. He was considered ruthless and feared in some circles, his wealth unmatched by most lords, his business empire vast and growing fast across the continent, and Lady Fanny had on more than one occasion reduced him to a stammering schoolboy. The mere memory had him scowling.

Though he did not like speculating about her like a gossip, he asked, "Did the rumor reveal the why of her actions?"

"No. But it is clear to me he dealt her an egregious insult. The rest of society only seems to be concerned that she *jilted* a marquess."

Sebastian's heart had yet to settle inside his chest, as his thoughts skipped from one notion to the other, all improbable and dangerous. He wanted to go to her, find a way to woo and court her. And he also wanted to give her time to recover from whatever had caused her to act without care of society's judgment. And he wanted to slay whoever had caused her hurt, but most of all he wanted to roar his triumph that she was no longer lost to him. A foolish desire to be certain for a genteel lady wasn't for the likes of him. He had a title now, but he was still the same coarse man in his thoughts, deeds, and friendships. Sebastian did not give himself the airs of gentility, he wouldn't even know how. His inaction before had seen her engaged to another when he had wanted her desperately. During their rare encounters over the past several months, his admiration had grown, but he had never shown it. This was providence.

He pushed from off the mat, prowled to the lone sofa in the corner of the room, grabbed a towel and raked it across his skin. With impatient motions he dried the sweat from his body, ignoring his friend's curious and mocking glance. "What do I do?" he asked, putting on a white shirt, and quickly making himself presentable before walking through that door. He had learned one did not cavort half-naked in front of servants.

"Do you really want my advice?" Percy asked quietly, his brown eyes unusually somber.

Sebastian pinched the bridge of his nose. "I want to call on her, but it would be outrageous for me to do so." *I'm making the same mistake as my old man.*

The intrusive and unwelcome voice had his thoughts careening to a terrifying halt. The first pause he'd had since the wicked need to claim Lady Fanny Dashwood commanded his regards.

His father had loved his mother with every emotion in his soul, and that man had died waiting for her to love him back. And Sebastian feared she never did, simply because his father had been a merchant and she had been the daughter of a country gentleman. He didn't think his mother had ever forgiven her family for marrying her off to a man so low in connections and education. Their marriage had been an odd one, certainly devoid of mutual love and respect, and while Sebastian had loved his mother, even as a child, he had seen the contempt she had for his father. A contempt born from the notion that she was his better in every way.

A rough sound issued from him. "I know what you are going to say, no need to repeat it."

Percy had been cautioning Sebastian against his admiration for Lady Fanny for months now. It wasn't possible for her regard to be returned, she was the daughter of an earl who had known her place in the glitter and pomp of high society since her birth. The thoughts he had of her in the nights, that illicit one of stripping her bare and splaying her across silken sheets while he feasted on her loveliness would never be realized.

"But will you heed my warnings?" Percy asked.

"For now," Sebastian murmured, walking away and out the door. He made his way to his study.

"So, you will not be epically foolish and rush over to Mayfair?" Percy demanded hurrying to catch up to him.

"I'm not a blathering idiot, nor am I insensitive to the privacy her family must require now."

"Ah…so you are retreating to plot your moves. How diabolical of you," he drawled.

Sebastian had no response to that, for that was precisely what he would do. Watch from the shadows and plot. He was being given a second chance, and he would not muck it up. Hell, he wasn't even sure what he wanted. To marry Lady Fanny Dashwood held vast appeal, but he was ever aware their union might turn out to be the misery that had been his parents' marriage. But Sebastian was not the type of man his father was. When he wanted something, it became the sole direction of his regard, and he did not believe in failure. If he had, he would have still been that boy struggling to emerge from the box society had placed him in.

"Will I see you later at Lady Marriot's ball?"

The very fact Sebastian got an invitation to the ball was only because Lord Marriot needed his money. They supposed he should be grateful to part from it because he had received a nod of approval from their lot. *Silly.* "No. I'll be working."

There were several meetings planned for the day, and he intended to take a tour of one of his iron factories in Leeds in the near future. He had bought several new machines, and his workers were frightened they would lose their livelihood. There were even murmurings of strike actions and union organization, and so he needed to take a walk through and quell those fears. Not that they were unfounded. Because the way of the world now was to use the best machinery to make businesses more profitable. But Sebastian could not in good conscience fire the workers who were becoming obsolete. A solution needed to be found, and there could be no delay.

The next few minutes were spent on business matters, and while he wanted to keep his mind on the task at hand, Sebastian couldn't help being distracted.

Lady Fanny Dashwood. A woman who was cultured, genteel, and pure. Everything he was not. But a woman who by a twist of fate he had not lost, and could not allow to slip from his grasp again.

❧

One week later…
Mayfair, London.

FANNY SAT on the windowsill in the drawing room and watched the trees dancing in the wind. The curtains were drawn, and the family was not available to callers. To Fanny, the somber atmosphere brought to mind when papa had died. The sleeting rains and horrid rumble of thunder did not help. Nor did the chilling disapproving distance her brother and mother maintained, nor the piercing pain that lingered in her. But why was she morose? It was not as if she had loved the marquess with her entire heart.

I thought I could. That had been enough for her. A promise of love, a promise of a family.

It still distressed her when she recalled that he had been so good-natured, and attentive. His few kisses had always been pleasant. In truth, it was the loss of something which she had hungered for that ripped through her with vicious claws.

Only a few days before, her future had seemed so clear and bright. She would have been the mistress of her own home, a husband she liked and respected, and children. Fanny fought the despondency that wanted to weigh her down.

"What are we to do?" Darcy, Countess of Banberry, demanded of her husband. "Fanny's reputation is in tatters, and it is affecting us all as a family. We cannot hope she will ever receive another respectable offer. It was bad enough when she jilted Lord Aldridge. But at least that was before they were at the altar. She ran away this time, with the whole of society looking on."

It was only one hundred pairs of judging eyes. More than enough to spread what they witnessed to the *ton*.

"The cloud of her disgrace will hover for years. And her actions have irrefutably harmed our position in society. I was not extended an invitation to Lady Prescott's annual garden party. That has never happened before, and I am beyond mortified."

Fanny turned from the windows and laced her fingers tightly before her. "Darcy…" A lump formed in her throat when her friend turned from her as if pained to look upon her. Since the debacle at St. George's Church, her sister in law, who had become her dearest friend, had not given her a chance to be heard. Nor had her brother. Her mother had been beside herself and promptly took herself off to their country estate in Hertfordshire.

Fanny had spent most of her time in her room, weeping at her crumbled dreams. Her brother had ignored her and had even sent a note she was not to join them for dinner and was to take a tray in her room. As if she were a petulant child being reprimanded. Fanny had ignored his edicts, but the terrible silence she had been treated to at the dinner table had encouraged her to eat alone since.

"She *must* marry immediately, but I cannot imagine who would have her now, so she must return to Hertfordshire and not show her face—"

Colin rapped his knuckles onto the small walnut table, and his wife's lips flattened. "Darcy, my love, if you will grant me a few minutes with my sister."

The countess flushed, lifted her chin, and exited the drawing room with quiet dignity.

Finally, he turned his regards to Fanny. Tears burned the back of her throat at the disappointment she saw in light green eyes very much like her own.

"I have been too angry with you to have this conversation before, Fanny. But I see now, it can no longer be delayed. What in the devil's name possessed you to run from committing to your vows and inciting such scandal and speculation into our lives? What possible justification could you have?"

Fanny had thought mamma told him. "There was something wrong," she whispered, a tight ache in her throat.

"Wrong?" her brother snapped. "*What* could possibly have been wrong? Lord Trent is imminently respectable, his estate is wealthy, and he has the ear of parliament, Fanny. How could you have been so foolish?"

In clipped tones, she told him what she saw.

Shock bloomed across her brother's handsome face, and he fisted his hands at his side. "You invited the ruin you are now facing because of a harmless embrace—"

She shot to her feet. "I am not a fool, brother, it was *not* a harmless embrace. Miranda Shelby is Lord Trent's mistress and seems to be with child." Fanny's voice cracked on that admission. "They have been together for ten years I have been told."

A flush ran along her brother's cheek. "How would you know of mistresses?" he demanded furiously. "That is something you needn't worry over. It is the way of the world for men to have mistresses. You would have been a marchioness, with an allowance that would give you the freedom to dabble in your passions, and you threw that all away for what?"

He came over, gripped her shoulders and shook her. "For what Fanny?"

"*Love*," she sobbed, the tears finally spilling. "I couldn't face a lifetime with Lord Trent knowing he held no esteem for me, and that the rumors saying he already has a woman he loves with his whole soul, but because of her lower status made her his mistress, were true. A life such as that would have been unbearable."

Her brother let her go and closed his eyes as if he couldn't bear looking at her. "You've ruined us for the stupid, idealistic notion of love."

Her stomach cramped. "No, I—"

"Can love provide you with fine clothes and carriages. Can it fill our pantries and place wages in our servants' pockets?"

She inhaled sharply. "Are we in dire straits?"

"No, we are not," he said tightly. "You could have been a marchioness, Fanny."

And there it was. The elevated dream her father and mother had long possessed for her. That their family would be aligned with the most powerful and noble bloodlines of the aristocracy.

"There is more to life than a title and more riches," she said quietly. "I believe—"

He scrubbed a hand over his face. "Not this poppycock again. Let me be clear. You have ruined your chances at any respectable alliance. You will not drag our family name through the mud again. Immediate marriage is what you need to render you respectable. I went back over all the men who've made an offer for you at your come out and wrote to—"

"You didn't," she cried, humiliation crawling through her. "How could you act in such a despicable manner?"

He shot her an incredulous glare. "I daresay you are confusing our actions. I am attempting to render you respectable. If that is at all possible. Earl Wyndham is willing to marry you post haste."

An image of their fat, balding neighbor in Hertfordshire, who was old enough to be her father…perhaps her grandpapa floated through her thoughts. "He is decrepit." Though actually, he was a very kind soul who had always made her feel at ease. As the largest landowner in their village, Fanny had been invited to several balls and picnics hosted by the earl. He was charming and rather amiable, but she had no desire for him. Lord Wyndham had always treated her like a daughter, and the very thought of the earl trying to kiss her was alarming to her nerves.

Colin's eyes went cold as if he sensed she would not fall in line with his plans.

"Do not be melodramatic, he is six and forty, hardly that old. And desires you despite your foolish behavior. I am doing what is best for you, Fanny."

She tried to maintain an air of dignified calm. "By pushing me onto a man for whom I have no regards? Surely you can see such an action is what is best for you."

Her brother gently gripped her shoulder. "Look at me," he murmured.

He held her gaze, a disquieting sorrow burning in his eyes. "I've long known of your desire to have a family of your own. This is your chance for that family. It took three years after your last disgrace for a gentleman to propose to you. And a marquess came your way, Fanny. And you gave him up for romantic idiocy. No other man will have you, and I do not have the heart to have you under my roof for several more years until another suitor comes along."

She flinched, biting her tongue to prevent the cry of pain that almost tore from her. As it were, the tears burning in her throat spilled down her cheeks even harder. "You want to distance yourself from my scandal."

"The rumors call you the worse sort of flirt, leading on a man to only render his humiliation. This is the second time you've jilted a man." He prowled over to his desk and snatched up a crumpled newspaper and thrust it toward her. "Do you know what they're calling you? The double jilt. You are *ruined*. Darcy hasn't had a caller since this farce. And you have not extended an apology to the marquess or this family."

Her heart was a dull thud in her ear, and her mouth went dry. "I'm…I'm…" she closed her eyes. She could not pretend contrition. The marquess had been intimate with a lady only minutes before attempting to marry her. That man was the worst sort of scoundrel, and she would have withered away in their marriage. It hurt, somewhere deep inside that her family only seemed to care about their social status, and not the blow that was dealt to her pride and heart. "He has a mistress," she whispered. "I could not marry him, and I cannot apologize for protecting myself."

"All men have mistresses," Collin roared.

"Do you?" for she knew he loved Darcy with every emotion in his heart.

He stared at her as if he could not believe her gall, but something akin to guilt flitted across his face. Fanny had often remarked to her friends how much her brother doted on his countess. It had never occurred to her he might have a soiled dove in his keeping. Her stomach cramped that he too might act with such dishonor and disregard for his wife's sensibilities and the love she had for him. "Do you have a mistress, Colin?" she demanded.

Her brother took a breath, leashing his impatience, but he made no reply. Silence blanketed the library as she stared at him in disbelief.

A ragged breath filled with such pain sliced through the stifling air. She whirled around to see Darcy hovering on the threshold, her delicate hand resting at her throat. The eyes that peered at her husband were wide and questioning, filled with doubts, denial, and pain.

Colin dealt her a wrathful glare. "*Damn* you, Fanny."

The shock of her brother cursing her paled to the knowledge he must have a lover. *Dear God.*

A cry broke from Darcy's throat, and then she whirled about and ran. Colin dashed after his wife, calling for her to stop. With legs that trembled, Fanny made her way over to the windowsill and lowered herself on the small ledge, resting her forehead on the cool glass.

Everything was ruined, and she had no notion of how to escape the despair scything through her soul.

CHAPTER 3

Several hours later, the man who stepped through the front door of their townhouse was as dangerous and unpredictable as the heralding storm. Fanny faltered in the hallway, the roses she'd intend to place on the table in the drawing room, forgotten. She was too far away to discern the words forming on his sensually shaped lips. Their butler, Jeffers, took the man's coat, and top hat. Stripped of those distractions the body revealed was perfectly dressed and breathtakingly formed. She'd always thought so of Sebastian Rutledge, the new Lord Shaw, the man society had dubbed the iron king and her brother's friend.

As if he felt her improper assessment, his eyes— a fierce blue-gray of a winter storm—collided with hers, and the vase in her hands trembled. The strangest of heat darted through her body, and her heart quickened. She had never been able to understand her reaction to this man. It was not as if they socialized. Her brother had always been careful which of his friends he brought into close association with her, and Fanny fancied this was the closest she has been alone with Lord Shaw since they were introduced. And that had been a little over two years ago. He had never asked her to dance at the few balls he'd attended, nor was he ever seated close to her when invited to dinner because of his rank. But she had always been aware that he watched her although he thought he was discreet. His eyes upon her had always been confusing, for he made no effort to converse with her, and she, in turn, avoided him for his intensity was both alarming and intriguing.

He smiled in her direction and for several seconds her wits scattered. How positively charming it was. She was then obliged for civility's sake to return a warm smile at him and proffer a greeting. "Lord Shaw, how good of you to call. May I invite you to the fire in the drawing room?"

"Thank you," he murmured.

Fanny was painfully aware of the way his eyes

kissed her skin. Surely, he was out and about in society enough to understand his obvious admiration was rude, and vulgar…and so distressingly lovely. Confoundingly it soothed the sting to her pride and vanity from seeing the man she was about to marry caught in the throes of passion in another's arms. She handed the vase of flowers to the butler and ordered refreshments. Then she made her way to the drawing room, with the viscount on her heels. They entered, and she carefully ensured the door remained ajar.

A fire burned merrily in the grate and suspecting him to be chilled from being caught in the downpour, she invited him to sit on the sofa closest to the flickering flames. "I will inform Colin you've called Lord Shaw."

He winced slightly, and she got the impression he did not like the honorific. Possibly she was mistaken, who could resent being a lord, and with such comfortable estates as it had been rumored he had inherited?

"I was hoping for a moment of your time, Lady Fanny."

She lifted her eyes to his, quite astonished. "I beg your pardon; did you say of *my* time?"

There was a mocking glint in his blue-gray eyes,

which she would allow were beautiful. She would never describe him as classically handsome like many of the men in society. The harsh sensuality of his features left no room for elegance or refinement, but he was compelling with his chiseled cheekbones, square jaw, and dark slashing brows. He also had the blackest hair she had ever seen, as if darkness itself had painted it. How would it feel to touch? Soft? Or coarse like? A flush went through her at the inappropriate thought.

"Yes," he said mildly.

An oddly exhilarating thrill of anticipation swept through her. "You are not here to call on my brother?" she asked inanely.

An indecipherable emotion passed over his face. "I will speak with him, but I was hoping for your indulgence first."

Her eyes widened, and her mouth went dry. Was it her imagination that he appeared agitated? *Surely not.* The man before her was Sebastian Rutledge, a self-made man of great wealth who owned several iron smelteries and factories in England and had business interests on the continent. There had been much speculation by society about the extent of his worth, and they had been unable to assess it accurately for he took none into his confidence. Not even her brother. But he was a man of singular fashion, and his manner was as elegant and rich as a gentleman of society. Though no one had entirely forgotten that he had common breeding, it was his air of affluence and the viscountcy which made him somewhat acceptable to her mamma and most in society.

"What could you have to say to me?" she asked lowering herself into a sofa.

He sat opposite her, on the very edge of his padded chair, as if he were impatient. "I..." he closed his eyes briefly, and she couldn't help noticing how incredibly long his lashes were...and this close, she could see the calluses on his palm and fingertips. It occurred to her then how much his gentleman like attire was a thin veneer of gentility.

"I am not very good at this," he said gruffly. "I have never done this before."

"Forgive me, my lord, I've no notion what you are about."

"You've had a bad run of it."

There could be no mistaking his meaning. She flushed, and he grimaced, no doubt accurately deducing that whatever he was about, he was making a hash of it.

"I've heard the whispers about your name that insist your reputation is beyond repair."

She flinched at his lack of delicacy.

He stilled, his expression impenetrable. "Forgive my bluntness. The thing to do is marry with all haste, and I—" he raked his fingers through his dark hair.

She had always thought him a man of few words, and her suspicion was proven. There was a hollowness forming in her stomach, for he had still managed to communicate he was here because of the odious cloud hanging over her head. Fanny shot to her feet, and he stood, and moved alarmingly close.

"Fanny…forgive me, Lady Fanny." His eyes caught hers, and she was unable to look away. "Would you do me the honor of marrying me?"

For a long moment, Fanny could only stare at him as if he were an apparition from one of Mrs. Radcliffe's gothic novels. She was of the opinion he could not be sincere. "I beg your pardon?"

"I believe you comprehended me, my lady."

"Bu-but you asked me to *marry you*!"

There was a bewildering mix of arrogance and wariness in his eyes. "I did."

Fanny was rendered speechless. "Without the

benefit of courtship?" she was uncertain why she asked the question for there could be no contemplation of his outrageous offer. They hardly knew each other.

"Do you want courtship? I never imagined you would since you have been through it twice already, to repeat it must be unpalatable."

How oddly fascinating they were having this conversation. "You are in earnest, my lord?"

His mouth tilted a little at one corner. "I am Lady Fanny. I also find I do not wish for you to slip through my fingers again and I must act with more haste than what is considered proper."

Her eyes widened. He had never expressed the hope that they might become better acquainted. And now…marriage? Was he in want of a fortune? Though he did have a title to recommend himself to her family, she did not think his offer would be entertained. His background was too dubious, and his title did not render him wholly respectable. Why, he was hardly invited to the best drawing rooms or balls. And when he did appear, it was quite evident his presence incited speculation and uncivil rumors. More than once mamma had remarked she pitied the lady he would take to be his wife and had thought it better if he looked to secure an alliance with one of the many American heiresses who hankered for any title.

"I...I cannot marry you." Her instinctive rejection felt wrong.

He moved scandalously close, his eyes searching her face with studied intensity. Fanny almost expired when he reached up and tucked a strand of her hair behind her ear, his knuckle barely grazing her cheeks. That touch, so light it was scarcely a breath of sensation, pierced her like a well-aimed arrow.

"I ask you not to dismiss my offer without some consideration," he murmured. "At least sleep on it."

There was a peculiar weakness in her heart, and Fanny could do nothing but stare at him. Lord Shaw was sincere, and she was...*terrified*. She jolted as the awareness slithered through her. Not even when Lord Trent had offered for her had she felt this out of sorts, this *breathless*. An achingly terrifying sensation that she was powerfully attracted to Sebastian Rutledge tore through her. She went very still, hardly daring to breathe.

"What madness is this?"

She whirled about, her hand pressing against her chest. "My goodness, Colin, you startled me." Had he heard the viscount's absurd offer?

From the thundercloud brewing in her brother's eyes, she surmised he had. "Lord Shaw has come to call. I...I fear I have a previous engagement to attend," she said and winced at the blatant lie. Even Sebastian Rutledge would suspect they'd had no caller, but he had stolen her composure. "If you will both excuse me."

Without waiting for their reaction, Fanny hurried from the drawing room closing the door behind her. She leaned against it, unable to believe the last minute had taken place. She was about to move away when her brother's shocked tones floated in the air.

"Did you just make an offer for my sister?"

Fanny stiffened, turned around and shamelessly pressed her ear flat against the door. It was unforgivably rude to eavesdrop, but that was the least of her sins.

"I wanted to assess how she would feel about the notion before I approached you."

"You are not entirely serious?" her brother demanded.

"I've heard rumors that only fortune hunters will now offer for her hand, and that you are seeking suitors for her."

Fanny trembled in reaction to that unwelcome

news. How dare her brother act with such rank disregard for her feelings.

"I thought you would want better for your sister. There is even a bet at White's going that you are so desperate you will accept the first offer that comes your way." Lord Shaw's tone was questioning and throbbed with an undertone of emotion she did not understand. How she wished she was still in the room to see his eyes.

"I will check the book at White's when I next visit," Colin said stiffly.

She was being discussed in the clubs. The very idea had humiliation cramping through her stomach.

"What are your designs on my sister?"

The anger in her brother's voice was alarming.

"I would like to marry her," Shaw said unapologetically. As if he were not low in connections and birth, a businessman asking for the hand of an earl's daughter.

Her prejudice left a sour taste in her mouth, and she did not like that she was painted with the same brush as the rest of society. Fanny had never found him rude or inconsiderate. As it were, the very idea of any man who wasn't hunting a fortune asking for her hand in marriage after the calamity that was her reputation was preposterous. The notion that it was Sebastian Rutledge was even harder to comprehend.

"My sister is a lady with well-bred sensibilities," her brother said stiffly. "How dare you even think to approach me for her hand?"

She'd never heard her brother's voice so cold and dismissive. Fanny frowned, for she had thought Sebastian Rutledge, a friend of Colin's.

"I'm not hunting her fortune."

Then why do you want to marry me?

Wariness settled atop her shoulders. Then her brother asked it as well.

"Why are you offering for her, I know damn well you don't need her money. You are the man they call the Iron king for God sakes."

"My reasons are my own but know that my regard for her is most sincere."

That admission had the most peculiar longing welling inside of her. *Oh, Dear God.* She fell too quickly in the throes of love, and twice now because of that foolish sentiment she had been deceived of a man's character. Not that she thought she could love this man. But he had always made her feel so… so…*warm*, and just from a mere stare.

"My sister has too much delicacy of mind and

tender sensibilities to walk by your side. She is not a stranger to a life of elegance amongst society. She is a *lady of breeding*."

"And I, of course, am not a gentleman," came his flat reply.

"Despite the title, you are not. Surely you know this. I've heard rumors you've no formal education. I cannot believe you would think to ask it. What would a man like you know of fine manners and good breeding to provide my sister with the lifestyle to which she is accustomed?"

There was a tense silence, and then the door opened, startling her. Her cheeks heated, and she peered up into the eyes of Lord Shaw.

His lips quirked, and amusement glowed in his eyes. "Eavesdropping? How intrepid and unladylike of you Lady Fanny. I confess you surprise me," he murmured.

"Why do you want to marry me, if not for my fortune and my connections," she whispered.

His eyes searched hers, intent. "I daresay you've bewitched me, and I want you."

A shock went through her, hot and delicious. That response she'd not anticipated. *You've bewitched me, and I want you.* And suddenly she knew he wanted to do wicked and improper things with her.

Heat crawled up her neck, mortification gripping her.

No gentleman had ever, would ever be so forward with a lady. Though she was the one to enquire after his reason, he could have been more discreet in his utterances. Sebastian Rutledge was indeed no gentleman. Still, the raw and sincere desire she spied within his eyes and conveyed by his words had a feeling of alarm and excitement washing over her senses. Unable to proffer any reply, she spun around and strolled away. For a wicked intrigue had brewed within her heart and she would be foolish even to consider his unexpected proposal.

CHAPTER 4

It was with a sense of disbelief and trepidation, several days later, under the banner of darkness, Fanny pounded on the door of a most elegant townhouse in Berkeley Square. She lowered her hand after hammering the knocker once more, her gaze scanning the darkened street. A few gas lamps were lit, but the fog blanketing the air filled her with nervous tension. The noise of horses' hooves sounded, but no carriage appeared through the dense fog. A light rain misted the air, and Fanny tugged her coat closer, shivering at the slight chill. *Dear God, am I making the right decision?* Her actions overwhelmed the bounds of propriety and every expectation she had of her conduct, but she wouldn't be deterred. She had allowed her brother to dictate too much of her life because her living had depended upon him.

But no more. She was now the possessor of her fortune, all fifty thousand pounds of it, with an annuity of ten thousand pounds to be added over the course of ten years. She was an heiress. And distressingly she could not buy respectability or a husband. Not that she would want to marry a fortune hunter, such a man was not the kind she wanted to spend the rest of her life with. Dear God, no, she needed more, so much more.

Don't be a ninny, look what my quest for love wrought.

The door wrenched open, and a glowering Sebastian Rutledge peered down at her.

"I…I'd expected the butler," she stammered, all the well-crafted demands for entry she had practiced abandoning her thoughts.

He stiffened, his expressive eyes shuttering. Several seconds slid by, he only stared, and Fanny gathered she had shocked him. Who would have thought him to possess an elevated sense of propriety? Then she winced, for she knew how outrageous her actions were. The man considered her for several more painful seconds, then he glanced behind her to the black lacquered carriage with no visible coat of arms. "At least you were smart enough to travel in an unmarked coach. To what do I owe the honor of this unexpected visit?"

The man had no social graces. It was unseemly that he had her standing on his doorstep, even if the hour was distressingly inappropriate. "Will you oblige me by granting me an audience for a few minutes?"

He moved back and held the door wide. She stepped inside, quite shocked at the darkness. A door loomed in the distance, light spilling from beneath, and it was toward that beacon she walked. Where was his staff? Why was everything so silent when it was barely nine in the evening? A strange shiver darted through her as she acknowledged the foolhardiness of her impetuosity. Why hadn't she sent a note and asked for a meeting in Hyde Park? She faltered and shuddered when his chest caressed her back ever so slightly. He was so close. "Where is everyone?"

"I live alone."

How preposterous. "You've no servants?"

"I'm not of a mind to have the people who work for me to do so from dawn until midnight. I leave such grueling expectations for my betters," he drawled mockingly.

Her heart was beating too hard. Fanny wetted

her lips, fighting the urge to turn around and flee. *Stay true to your course.* Squaring her shoulders, she once again strolled toward that single light. They reached the door, and he reached around her and pushed it open for her. She crossed the threshold, grateful to see a merry fire burning in the grate, and several lit candles on the mantel and a large oak desk which dominated the center of the room. They were in his study then.

The door closed behind her with a decisive click and her mouth dried. He walked past her to lower himself at the edge of his desk, his muscled forearms also braced against the side. Fanny gawked, feeling faint. Lord Shaw's state of undress was alarming. His thick dark hair was disheveled. He wore no cravat or waistcoat, but a white shirt where the collar was unbuttoned showing the corded muscles of his throat. *Dear God.* His shirt was not tucked into his trousers, and the man had on no boots.

She glanced around the room to see boots discarded by the lone sofa near the fire, and his jacket, cravat, and waistcoat draped over the back of another chair.

She lifted the veil from her face. Fanny had

been cautious in disguising herself before she had left the comfort of her brother's townhouse.

"I had the greatest apprehension in coming here tonight," she said with a small smile, hoping to quell the tension that seemed to blanket the room.

His gaze rested thoughtfully on her face. "You should."

Fanny scowled. Why did he have to sound so ominous? What if he should ravish her before she left? A blush heated her face, and his eyes sharpened. It was as if he could read her every mortifying thought. The sudden slant of his mouth seemed almost…threateningly sensual.

She didn't want to get too close to the man, but Fanny succumbed to the lure of the fire and moved even further into the cozy study.

"I believe it may be prudent to remove your coat," he murmured. "I believe it to be damp."

There was a provoking dare in his eyes, one to which she hardly knew how to respond.

She untied the strings of her cloak, pushing back the hood from her face, Fanny reluctantly removed the garment. Those penetrating eyes dropped to her slender figure, and it wasn't her imagination that something indefinable darkened his gaze.

"Would you like a drink?"

"Yes," she said, grateful for the chance to hold onto something. Her hands shook, even when she laced them together.

He stood and moved to the sideboard. There was a clink as he tilted the bottle over two glasses. His movements were so graceful yet intimidating. She realized then he was a large man, the top of her head could be tucked under his chin. A certain ruthless strength characterized his demeanor. And it made her uncomfortable. He was not at all like any other gentleman she'd met or conversed with. Despite his acquaintanceship with Colin, her brother had been careful to keep the pair of them at a distance to each other.

A glass was pressed into her hand. "Thank you, my lord," she murmured.

He resumed sitting on his desk, and she wondered if it was her fanciful imagination that there was a disquieting anticipation in the gaze that settled on her. She took a sip of her drink, coughing slightly at the burn that warmed her insides. How had she not realized she was so cold.

"Now tell me why you would risk the little that is left of your reputation to come here, my lady."

She strolled over to the sofa which invited

repose and sat. Fanny met his regard steadily. "My brother believes I should marry right away and retreat to the country until the scandal surrounding my name has died down. He has found a man willing to marry me despite the stain on my name. The Earl of Wyndham, and he's a gentleman of rank and fortune, with an estimable bloodline and reputation."

She stared in fascination at the white-knuckled grip he had on his glass. It was a wonder it did not shatter.

"So, you are once again engaged?"

"I've refused," she said softly.

A breathless silence blanketed the library. Then he cleared his throat. "Why?"

"I want the man I marry...the man I will spend the rest of my life with to be *my* choice." That need had become a hollow, painful ache. "The man my brother selected is very kind and charming, and while I quite like him, he is old enough to be my father and already has six children."

"I see. And how has this awareness led you to me at this hour?"

The predatory hunger that emanated from him made her unaccountably expectant, except for what she was undecided.

"While I am fond of Lord Wyndham, I daresay he will not make me a good husband. He has one foot in the grave, and I am certain the only reason he wants to marry me is so that I can be there for his brood of children. While I desire children of my own, I...I think it may be best if I start out with one and not six. My brother cannot seem to understand this and is planning a wedding without a care for my feelings."

Her voice cracked, and she waited for a few beats to gather her composure. The quarrels she had been having with her brother had been making her life miserable. He had the gall to blame her for the distance between himself and Darcy. And most dreadful of all, she could not help feeling her brother wanted to be rid of her. Fighting back another wave of sadness she continued, "I am certain he expects me to obediently fall into line because he knows my heart desires, you see. And he is cruelly playing on my fears."

Lord Shaw had not moved, but his intensity increased. "And what is your heart's desire?"

"Once it had been for a grand love."

"You no longer desire this?"

She drew a breath that felt, and sounded, unsteady. "My wants are now more rooted in reality and not for frivolous and unlikely sentiments. I desire to be the mistress of my own home, freedom to dabble in my passions. I paint seriously when I am in the country, and I do so enjoy riding. I should like to have children, and the sooner, the better. I am on the cusp of being three and twenty, and I cannot wait for society to forgive another slight. *That* may take another three years."

His expression shuttered. "I see."

She folded her hands in her lap. "As it were, you are the only other man who dared to call at the house since…well, you *know* what. But my brother does not approve of you."

There was a decidedly dangerous gleam in his gaze. "And you do?" he asked smoothly.

I dreamed of you, kissing me. Of course, she would never admit that, but Fanny had been shocked to find herself thinking of him at every moment of the day. "I approve enough to accept your offer of marriage if you are so inclined," she said hoarsely, wings of fright and doubt beating in her heart.

He went still—utterly and entirely still.

Oh, please say something, she cried silently when he only stared.

"I should count myself happy, Lady Fanny, to be able to call you my wife. I will stipulate I will not wait. There will be no courtship or long engagement. I want you."

And at that moment, Fanny suspected he was exerting an enormous amount of will not to ravish her. She couldn't decide if she should be frightened or thrilled, but it was positively wonderful to be desired.

A roaring began in her head. "Our union would be one of convenience, my lord." A legal union with no promises of love. There would be no dashed expectations on her part if they understood from the beginning what was anticipated. Pain squeezed her insides. The very idea of infidelity made her feel faint. "I would…"

"Yes?"

She swallowed. "I know it a strange thing to ask, but I would demand your fidelity. *Always*."

Those eyes that saw far too much roved over her face. An odd expression lit his eyes. He would never be able to appreciate the extraordinary willpower it took to maintain his regard.

"But not my adoration?"

That soft question did frightfully strange things to her inside. Her breathing quickened, and unfamiliar heat darted low in her stomach. He prowled over to her, and she stood, peering up at him. Fanny swallowed. "I too am not interested in an engagement period." She would probably be overcome and change her mind if she tarried. "I would like to be married by the end of the week by special license. I do hope you can procure one."

A small smile tipped his lips at her evasion. She did not know how to respond. Would there ever be a time she would want his love? Chasing that idea had seen her almost married to a fortune hunter, and then to a libertine. Both men hadn't truly wanted her and would never have tried to learn her heart. How easily words of love and flattery had fallen from their deceitful lips. Fanny refused to fool herself any longer. Marriages were business transactions, a trade, where they benefited each other and perhaps in time affection would grow if the heart was inclined. Her brother hadn't married Darcy because he loved her but because he had been found kissing her. Thank heavens it was Darcy's mother who had discovered them in the conservatory, but they had been forced to wed despite Colin's protestations. Two years later Fanny could have said with confidence he loved his wife and Darcy worshiped him with her eyes. But now it seems he too had a mistress, shattering Fanny's certainty that he loved his wife infallibly. So, she had no real example that the kind of love she sought existed.

Perhaps in time, she would come to love this man, and he would feel the same. Especially if he was true to his word and remained devoted to her. She almost snorted. Sebastian Rutledge did not seem the sort for falling into the throes of passion and reciting sonnets. Except, she had no idea what this man wanted from her.

"I had thought to give you a month to prepare. Why the haste?"

You will be married by the end of the month, Fanny. I want you from under my roof and in your own home.

Even now the harsh words spoken by her brother only a few hours past seemed lodged in her soul. "Though I do not want to believe it of him, I fear Colin may do something underhand to see me wed to Lord Wyndham."

Dark shadows moved across Mr. Rutledge and her apprehension increased.

"My fears may be unwarranted," she hurriedly assured, somehow understanding this man would be wrathful if any harm came to her. The absurd notion warmed deep inside. "I must also warn you my brother is the trustee of my inheritance. He may never release it to me if we wed."

"And what is this amount?"

"Fifty thousand pounds upon my marriage or on my five and twentieth birthday. An unentailed cottage in Derbyshire. A misnomer really, for it boasts fifty rooms and sits on several acres with a splendid lake. And an annuity of ten thousand pounds for ten years."

"I will double all of that when we marry as your marriage portion."

His generosity and the wealth it implied shocked Fanny. He stood and strolled over to her then he cupped her cheek, and she trembled. "Lord Shaw, I—"

He placed a thumb against her lower lip, exerting the slightest pressure until her lips parted. A small thrill swept through her. His purpose seemed to be ravishment. The awareness stirred a small bit of anxiety and intrigue. She leaned closer, allowing his warmth to surround her.

"Sebastian," he murmured, dipping his head and pressing his lips to hers.

The fleeting touch of his lips to hers was a shock to her senses. *Sebastian*. His name whispered through her heart in an intimate caress, and her senses careened as he held her in an embrace that was far too intimate. He held her to his chest, and the soft, material of her gown slid sensually against her skin. She could not pull away, and Fanny allowed him to tighten his embrace and drag her up to his body for a deeper kiss. She gasped at the soft feather-like pressure of his lips against her. His embrace was fierce, unyielding, and she shivered at the sensations rioting through her.

Something curious, hot, and sweet stirred in her veins. And all at once, Fanny felt bewildered but exhilarated.

Oh, what am I doing?

The chaotic desires that peaked in the low of her stomach were surely unladylike and wanton, but she was unable to stop herself from falling helplessly into his kisses.

CHAPTER 5

Sebastian wanted to shout his triumph when Fanny's lips parted after the sweetest sigh of surrender. A small noise broke from her throat, curiously soft, filled with wonderment and pleasure.

Then her taste hit him, spice and sweetness, and his entire soul stirred. For a moment, he felt thoroughly disoriented, drunk on the flavor of her mouth. He framed her delicate face with both hands and slanted his lips over hers with a far greater passion than he had planned. He coaxed her lips even wider, and then dipped his tongue into heaven. He kissed her with ravishing expertise.

She whimpered. The sound made him go still. Finally aware he must be bruising her tender mouth with his passions, he took a deep breath. And released her lips.

Her green eyes had widened and darkened with shock. Her lips were red and swollen. A deep flush worked up from the collar of her dress to the edge of her hairline.

"Lady Fanny," he began gruffly. *Christ.* He hardly knew where to start. She was a lady, and he had taken a kiss from her like she was a doxy.

Trembling fingers rose to touch her swollen lips, and when he reached for her, she jerked away. That rejection was like a fist to his gut, and he stilled. She moved away from him, facing the fire, and he could see the slight tremble in her elegant frame.

"I never meant to lose control, I—" he cursed silently.

A great hush fell upon the room.

It hardly mattered he had only wanted to kiss her, it was evident to him he had frightened her with his coarse manners. "I apologize for my untoward behavior." What the hell was he thinking to even want to marry her? He wasn't a gentleman, he wasn't genteel with his desires. How would he even consummate their marriage? The way he made love, licking and tasting a woman all over, splitting her legs wide to suck along her sex until her taste exploded on his tongue, her cries of bliss echoing in his ears, and then…and only then would he ride them long and hard to completion. This seemingly delicate woman before him wouldn't even be able to tolerate him seeing her nakedness. She would possibly think their marriage bed an indignity she must suffer, much like his mother had.

The thought lingered, troubling him.

He was a damn fool.

Then she turned "There is no need to apologize." Her face flushed a delicate, rosy hue. "I…I simply had no notion it was possible to be kissed like that."

The most delightful color blushed on her face. "And we are affianced, so some enthusiasm is expected."

The tension winding through his soul eased.

Lively intelligence glittered in her exotically slanted eyes. "I must ask, Lord Shaw…Sebastian, why do you wish to marry me?"

In those beautiful eyes, lingered an aching demand, one that begged for sweet words and praises, and it struck him that she did want words of love, but perhaps no longer trusted in it. As it were, he did not love her. It was impossible. Sebastian wasn't even sure what love felt like. But he wanted her in his bed, by his dinner table. She would add more than a refinement to his life, she would be the proof he had achieved all he had ever hungered for.

"I am eight and twenty years, and I have been thinking to marry. Since I met you…Fanny, you rouse hunger in me unmatched by any other."

Her eyes widened, and she blushed prettily speaking of innocence that made him feel far too worldly for her. He wondered if any of the ladies he knew blushed.

"I've also wanted to marry a lady of quality."

She canted her head to the side and seemed to think on that. "You are accepted in society."

"Barely," he said flatly. "I am tolerated. With a wife of your breeding and connections, I daresay my low origins will become more palatable when they rub elbows with me."

Compassion and something more glittered in her eyes. "Thank you for being honest."

Sebastian couldn't help feeling as if he had wounded something tender inside of her. He cleared his throat. "Please do not mistake me. I've had a few other offers from families of quality."

They had needed his fortune, and a couple of the daughters had acted most ridiculously to sway his interest. He had never been the type of man to succumb to force or blackmail. If he had been that weak of character, the world would not now call him the Iron King, and scurry to be in his favor.

"Yes, I did hear the rumor that Lady Arabella tried to compromise you. She is the daughter of an earl and had a blemish-free reputation, marriage to her would benefit you more."

"Possibly," he said, smiling when she scowled. Evidently, he should not have agreed, women were such contrary creatures. "But it is not her I've ever dreamed of kissing."

Lady Fanny brightened visibly. "I will speak with Colin and inform him—"

"I will be the one to meet with your brother. Return home, and I will call upon him in the morning."

She lifted her chin defiantly. "No. He needs to hear this from me. I would like to speak with him first."

Her courage was a thing to behold. Ladies of quality did not hie themselves off to bachelors' lodgings in the middle of the night to decide their own futures and then merely inform their family they were to marry. Colin would try and browbeat her into a life she did not want. He would probably have her carted off to the country or some other nonsense. Sebastian would not allow his friend to abuse her gentle spirits. "If that is your wish, please, by all means, speak with him."

She gasped. "Truly?"

How much that question revealed. Before him stood a young lady much used to her will and desires being decided for her.

"Truly," Sebastian murmured.

A radiant smile burst on her lips. "Thank you, Sebastian. Now I must go."

He helped her into her coat, keenly aware that her delightful scent of lavender stole into his lungs. How he wanted to gather her close and kiss her again. For so long he had starved for a taste of her, had hungered to see her walking beside him, to dance with her. His mind still had not accepted that she would soon be his. A sense of strangeness had embraced him and was not of a mind to let him go. She seemed so different from him, so much softer and refined. Even the way in which she spoke, her accent was clipped, and her vowels drawn out. The hint of elusiveness fascinated him, and he wondered if he wanted her so much because she had seemed so unattainable.

"You will not regret your decision," he said, vowing to treat her like the lady she was, always. He would need to govern his appetites once they wed and ensure the ugly side of his business never marred her in any way.

☙❧

THE VERY NEXT MORNING, Fanny joined her brother and Darcy in the small breakfast room. The rains had finally halted, and the day promised to be filled with sunshine and hope. Perhaps she could coax Darcy to ride with her along Rotten Row in the afternoon. Though it was unlikely her friend would desire to go out when they would be the butt of sly glances and speculative whispers. There was also a strain around her friend's mouth she did not like, it spoke of an unhappiness Fanny had never witnessed in her before. And she feared it had been caused by her blunder in demanding whether her brother had a mistress.

They ate cinnamon bread, scrambled eggs, kippers, and roasted ham in silence. Colin at times stared at his wife, and she ignored his presence as if he were an ant. They did not speak with Fanny, caught up in their silent battle. Polishing the last of her bread spread with raspberry jam, she leaned back in the well-padded chair. "I have some news."

Her brother managed to wrest his gaze from his wife to her. "I hope it is good tidings."

"I am afraid it will be disagreeable for you," she said quietly.

That got Darcy's attention, and she lowered her knife to stare at Fanny.

Darcy gave her an expectant look. "What news is this, Fanny?"

"I'm to be married."

Her brother nodded approvingly. "I'm relieved you are reconciled to accepting Lord Wyndham. He—"

"I'll be marrying Viscount Shaw."

Her brother slowly lowered his knife. "I beg your pardon?"

"I've accepted his offer of marriage."

"What could have possessed you? That damn bounder dared to approach you behind my back and—"

"I went to him…"

Fanny could not ever recall a time her brother appeared so astonished.

"Your conduct goes beyond the line of what may be tolerated, Fanny. To proposition the man?"

She delicately spread jam on a slice of toast. "You have been trying to decide my future when you had the privilege to do so for yourself. Though you were compromised with Darcy, you were already halfway in love with her. I do not wish to marry Lord Wyndham. I've heard you say on more than one occasion that Sebastian Rutledge is a man of exceptional qualities."

He scowled in evident frustration. "For a businessman, but he is beneath *you*."

Sadness pierced her. "Do you truly believe this?"

His closed expression spoke for him.

Her hand tightened on the handle of the knife. "Why?"

"He *works*," her brother said furiously. "He has spat on his title and his position in society repeatedly since he inherited his title. He does not conduct himself like a gentleman, and that is because he was not raised as one. You marrying such a man cannot be better than marrying an earl. As a countess, you will be better placed—"

"Forgive me, Colin. I do not mean to interrupt. I believe even you have conferred with the viscount on investment matters. I daresay his acumen for business matters is something to be praised not vilified. It could be argued that any man who works to build his wealth and profession is superior to a man who inherited his fortune and hardly knows what it means to sweat for anything. I cannot perceive that somehow we are above him in any way." She took a calming breath.

"Dear God," her brother muttered, glaring at her. "You are entirely serious. Mamma will be driven to her bed when she hears of this. You've always been so high-spirited."

Fanny winced. "I thought never to marry and live under your roof until I claim my inheritance. But I can see that is not to happen. You want me gone," she said softly. "Though it pains my heart, I must accept your wishes."

Guilt flashed in his eyes. "I will not release your fortune if you marry someone I do not approve of."

"Your management of the trust my money is held in will expire on my five and twentieth birthday. I daresay I can wait until another two years to come into my inheritance fully. Viscount Shaw has an astonishing amount of money, and I already suspect he will be indulgent."

Her brother scowled, and Fanny smiled, though

there was little to be amused about, for a moment she felt pleased that she had ruffled his feathers. "I never meant to embarrass this family when I ran from the altar. Lord Trent hurt my heart and dashed my hopes, and I am happy I was not persuaded to marry a man who has so little regard for me. Please be happy with my decision. I wish not to part from you with bitter feelings between us."

Colin's expression softened. "And you think Sebastian Rutledge has tender sentiments for you?"

She recalled the heat in his eyes, the firm press of his lips to hers, the passion that had blazed through her soul. "No, I am not entirely sure what he feels for me. But I am not deceived into any false expectations of what our marriage will be like. It will be one of convenience and mutual respect," she said quietly.

"I had not the smallest suspicion you could be so intractable," her brother finally said.

Looking up, she mustered a smile. "Then will you give your blessings?"

"He is very unrefined, Fanny," he said, clearly trying to deter her still. "Shaw is wealthy to be sure, but I cannot see how you will be happy with a man who exists in a world so far from the elegant life to which you are accustomed. He mixes with stage people, actors, and actresses, one of his closest friend is a doctor I'm told, and another of his business partners used to be a pugilist. They are all common, and he has made no effort to repudiate them and move into more genteel society. I daresay you will be expected to mix with their society as well. Such a notion cannot possibly be welcomed."

She flushed, hating the worm of doubt filling her veins. "It isn't likely I shall ever receive another offer. I cannot wait years for society to welcome me again."

Darcy offered her a small compassionate smile, her eyes no longer cold and distance. "Please do not be hasty. Let's talk as sisters and devise another plan. Surely the earl may be a better option than Shaw, Fanny?"

"No…he isn't."

"For heaven sakes, why not?"

*Because Sebastian makes me feel…*She pushed back her chair and stood. "Because Viscount Shaw is my choice. We are to marry by special license, and I would be pleased if you both attend. If you will excuse me, I will start my packing today and pen a letter to mamma."

Then she walked from the dining room, into the

hallway and up the stairs. Her orderly, well-planned life had been turned upside down and Fanny was curiously unafraid. Perhaps she was too foolish not to feel any sort of apprehension, or the intrigue that had long burned in her heart had eclipsed all else.

No, I shan't be afraid…for once I'll live by my desires.

CHAPTER 6

One week later…

I am *Viscountess Shaw.*

The well sprung carriage that she traveled in rattled along the cobbled streets taking her from her brother's townhouse in Mayfair to her new home in Berkeley Square. Her trunks, portmanteau, valises, and hat boxes had been packed and sent on early in the morning, but it had only been two hours since Fanny had vowed before God, the bishop, her brother, and Darcy that she would cherish and obey Sebastian Rutledge. How had she not realized that obeisance was a part of marriage vows, she had scowled at that bit and hesitated. Sebastian had been amused and had bent and whispered in her ear that he did not expect it of her. Fanny wasn't sure if that revealed the kind of man who thought of others beyond himself and did not believe in slavish adoration or did he perceive her to be the intractable and quarrelsome sort. She hoped it was not the latter. That was not a good opinion a husband should have of his wife.

She pushed aside the curtains to see they were now on Davies Street. In a few minutes, she would arrive at her new home and the anxieties attacking her were severely unwelcome. *Oh, dear what was I thinking?* And why was it *now* she was feeling doubts? The past few days she had felt a sense of relief that she would soon be in her own home, away from the loving restrictions of her brother. She hadn't dreaded the thought of sharing a home with Lord Shaw, but now her nerves were stretched thin simply because she could not imagine what their life would be like.

As a marchioness, her role would have been clear. Produce an heir and a spare as soon as possible. And though the notion stung that the marquess would have valued her womb far more than her witty intellect and company, that was the way of their world. She would have expected to run their household and organize the staff with graceful efficiency, plan balls, contribute to charities, and host dinner parties. Sebastian Rutledge had a title, but he wasn't a gentleman at all. What was she supposed to do as his wife? What kind of people would she be called upon to entertain? Where would they live when the season ended? What would be expected of a woman whose husband owned iron foundries? Did he too want an heir and a spare like all the other lords? He hadn't been reared with that expectation to duty and his bloodlines, and the awareness she truly had no notion of the character of the man she had wed had been driven through her heart like a stake.

Fanny felt distressed that she was only *now* thinking about those matters. Well in truth these worries had started the night before when she had stared into the canopied curtain above her bed. She had risen with the sun and prepared for her wedding day with mixed emotions of relief and uncertainty.

Fanny had worn her most fashionable dress, and delight had burned in her veins at his all-encompassing stare. To her mind, his regard had been too direct and intense, and anyone would think the man had already compromised her virtue.

The wedding breakfast at her brother's home

had been filled with forced joviality, and she had been delighted indeed when it had been over. The most mortifying memory had been when Darcy had taken Fanny into the private parlor and tried to impart to her what her duties as a wife involved in the marriage bed since her mother had not elected to attend.

She had written her mother of the news of her engagement to Sebastian, and she had only replied that she was prostrate with disappointment over her daughter's choice, and when her nerves had recovered, she would return to town. For now, she would take to the waters of Bath. Fanny had decided to leave her mother's disappointment and acceptance to time, seeing it would take a while for her mother to recover from losing a marquess as a son-in-law.

She knew little about men and the intimacies expected in marriage. Somehow Fanny hadn't imagined she would be expected to reveal her naked body to her husband. Her shock had been so great she had almost fainted. She knew there was to be some kissing of course but nothing much after.

Since her talk with Darcy, Fanny had existed in an acute state of mortification at her ignorance and worse she did not believe she could appear in the nude before a man she hardly knew and allow him to touch her. According to Darcy, he would do more than touch and Fanny was perturbed. Her sister in law said Colin had protected her delicate nature as much as possible and controlled his base urges. What that meant Fanny had no notion, but the implication that because her husband was not a gentleman, he would not be mindful of her sensibilities was strong.

The carriage rumbled to a halt, and a quick peek through curtains revealed they were at 57 Berkeley Square. The door was opened, and she allowed her husband who had elected to ride beside the carriage to assist her down.

"I trust your journey was pleasant?"

How polite he was. "It was. I do think it could have been better if you had been in the carriage." The soft admonishment in her words was inescapable.

His mouth curved ever so slightly. "I believe I was granting you the privacy of your thoughts."

She placed her hand on his and walked with him up the few cobbled steps. Her new home was grand and one of the more modern townhouses built. The house had a stone façade and climbed four stories above the lower ground floor. It faced onto Berkeley Square Gardens and had a pretty view from the front windows of a beautiful Grecian style statue of a half-draped lady carrying a large water vase. When they arrived at the door, Fanny was surprised to see Sebastian fishing for keys to open the door.

Where was the butler?

He allowed her to precede him inside a most elegant entrance hall. Footsteps echoed, and a sturdy woman hurried toward them, her face wreathed in smiles.

"Mr. Rutledge, sir I was not expecting you back so soon."

Why did she call their lord mister? The lack of proper address was shocking.

Fanny tugged off her bonnet, and Sebastian assisted her from her coat.

"Mrs. Campbell, may I present my wife, Mrs. Fanny Rutledge. Fanny Mrs. Campbell is my housekeeper."

Fanny smiled, and Mrs. Campbell dipped into a surprisingly graceful curtsy.

"It's a right pleasure to meet you, milady. I've baked a fruitcake for the occasion and prepared all your favorite dishes, Mr. Rutledge."

Sebastian politely declined, and Mrs. Campbell

hurried away, muttering about sending tea to the drawing room. Fanny peeked at him from beneath her lashes. He was looking down the hallway, a frown splitting his brows. They stood there for several seconds, not speaking or moving.

She gave him a questioning glance. "Is all well, Sebastian?" An unusual warmth unfurled through her at the intimate use of his name.

He glanced down, and it was then she noticed how vivid and beautiful the shards of blue in the unfathomable silver of his eyes were. During their brief ceremony, she had made a concentrated effort to stare at his nose. How silly she had been.

"I find I am confounded about what to do with you."

Her lips parted on an inelegant gasp. "I beg your pardon?"

"I've never had a wife before." His voice held a gently mocking note. At himself?

Fanny was flustered. She glanced at the hallways clock, noting it was barely one in the afternoon. Then she huffed a breath. "Well, *I've* never had a husband before." When her world had been scandal free, at this time, she would be walking the grounds of their country manor, calling on neighbors or attending a picnic with friends.

Their gazes collided, and the humor in his pulled a light laugh from her. "We are absurd," she gasped.

"That we are," he murmured.

A strange thrill of sensation tore through her. He was so large, masculine and beautiful.

"Perhaps you will allow me to give you a tour of your new home?"

Fanny smiled, unable to explain the way her heart started to pound. Unable to prevent herself, she tugged her gloves off and pinched her inner wrist.

A devastatingly slow and sensual smile slanted his lips. "I'm afraid it is real. We are married."

She felt an overwhelming pull between them, and her thoughts invariably turned to their wedding night. She didn't need to glance down at her palm to know her entire body had flushed scarlet.

There was a flicker of challenge in his eyes. "I must know the thought that provoked you to blush so becomingly."

"No, a lady's thoughts are her own, and it is not gentlemanly of you to ask after them," she said primly.

On odd expression marred his face to vanish quickly.

"It is very unusual that we are just standing here."

He laughed, and it rippled through her.

"I like that you laugh," she said softly, then blushed for having said it aloud.

"I like that you are my wife."

Fanny didn't know how to reply. The possessiveness stamped in his face had a peculiar disquiet slicing through her. Was it that he only saw her as a coveted prize? Unexpectedly his head dipped, and a fleeting kiss brushed against her lips. His mouth tugged at hers, his teeth lightly grazing her lower lip.

He lifted his head and considered her for several seconds as if he were trying to ascertain what to do with her at this moment. A flash of intuition went through her. The dratted man was thinking of her carnally. She ruthlessly fought the blush, unaccountably not wanting to appear gauche. Fanny stepped around him, trying her best to remain outwardly unaffected. Inside she was burning with heat and uncertainty. *This must be desire.*

Sebastian proceeded with the tour of her new home. It was a palatial townhouse even more so than her brother's, boasting over a dozen rooms. The ground floor held a large and elegantly appointed drawing room, a smaller parlor stylishly decorated, a library, Sebastian's study, and an impressive ballroom that opened onto small gardens. There was a large room on the lower floors designated as an exercise room where he'd blithely informed her he boxed and fenced with his friends. She'd never heard of any house having such a room, since one could join Gentleman Jackson's boxing academy on Bond Street, but she had not commented. Fanny was so used to conforming to society's standards, she felt a startled rush of pleasure that he was so very different. It hinted at mysteries to unlock and layers of his character to discover.

The upstairs boasted seven bedrooms, and she had been pleased to see she had her private chamber. Though the connecting door had loomed threateningly. But the thing that had given her the most pleasure was the music room with a masterpiece of a grand piano. Though she loved to sing, her skill at the pianoforte was lackluster at best, and she was still glad for it. He had taken her up through the servant stairs, and down to the kitchens where she had met the cook, the housekeeper and another maid and a footman. Disconcertingly they all referred to him as mister.

Now almost an hour later, Sebastian had bid her farewell, and Fanny reclined on the bed, her feelings bewildered. She truly had no notion what marriage to Sebastian Rutledge would be like. But she was now the lady of her own home, which, though beautiful, was understaffed, for she had no intention of opening her own front door whenever she was called upon by whomsoever should come calling. Everything about her marriage was strange and unfamiliar but being a lady of the house was a recognizable role, and one she would delve into as an aid to cope with her new situation. A situation whose greatest trial was just a few hours away. She was not prepared, knew not how to prepare. All Fanny could do was wait for the drumming of her racing heart to slow and for her new husband to show her what he expected of her...

⚜

THE FEEL of the piano keys under the tips of his fingers grounded Sebastian. Then his fingers glided over the smooth ivory, and it was as if he saw the music dancing in the air as the keys came alive.

Dinner had been over for almost two hours, he had taken a bath and then succumbed to the lure of the music room and a glass of brandy in the hopes of stifling the uncertainty burning through his gut.

It was laughable. *He* was uncertain. Why in God's name? All he had to do was mount those damnable stairs, open the connecting door, and take his wife…his sweet, beautiful and utterly charming wife in his arms, kiss her, ravish her, and make her irrevocably his.

Except he had never been with a virgin before, or a woman as delicate as Fanny Dash…*Rutledge* or was it, Viscountess Shaw? With a soft grunt, he sat before the grand piano and played. He allowed the music to be the balm that soothed his soul, to temper his hunger, and to transport him away from the cruel demands pummeling his body.

For two years he had resisted even thinking of her carnally, not wanting to dishonor her with his lurid imaginations, but now that she was his, wicked ideas of how he wanted to love her twisted through his mind.

He pounded away at the keys, losing his finesse, closing his eyes, seeing her as he wanted, naked, splayed wantonly atop pristine white sheets, her golden hair splayed across the pillows, her pale complexion in stark contrast, and her legs parted in welcome.

It was improbable that he should hear any noise above the music he made, but he stilled.

"You play so beautifully," his wife said, hovering in the doorway. There was an uncertainty in her voice he perceived to be uncommon for her. He couldn't face her, didn't want to. Dinner had been such torture, and more tension-filled than he'd expected. There had been a knowing in her gaze, and it had disconcerted him to see fright as well.

And then awareness had settled in his gut. She anticipated their wedding night. It was his duty and his privilege to consummate their vows, yet there was an unexpected hesitation in his heart. His fingers trembled over the keys creating a discordant note. Sebastian quickly caught the note, and he played, pushing away the knowledge of how close she stood, losing himself in the music spilling from his fingertips. A few moments passed, then shock punched through him when the most beautiful voice he'd ever heard filtered on the air. It was then he turned around, unable to believe notes so powerful and pure could come from someone so delicate.

Her song ended abruptly, and her color heightened.

"That was amazing, Fanny."

She smiled tentatively. "I simply thought I ought to share a bit of me as well."

He hadn't the heart to tell her he hadn't been sharing with her when he played but had been ignoring her. Sebastian supposed one should never tell a wife or a woman they could be ignored, for as he had heard so often, ladies' vanities should be flattered, and the prettiest of compliments should be paid.

The few lovers he had taken hadn't required sweet words or praises. They reveled in their sensuality and would have accosted him even before dinner. They would have fondled his cock before sucking him to completion, then moved onto the main course. In his wicked fantasies, his wife always appeared the temptress, seductive, but Fanny glowed with innocence and shyness. And he did not know how to seduce her. What if he couldn't be gentle enough? If he had any decency, he would send her away this very moment.

"Would you like a drink, Fanny?"

"Oh, yes please." Her smile wobbled, and she

glanced around the room, doing her utmost not to meet his gaze.

Sebastian pushed from the bench, and moved over to the mantle, and grabbed the bottle of brandy he had taken in earlier. "Do you drink brandy?"

Her eyes widened. "I've never had it."

"I confess I am uncertain if I will offend you by offering it."

She smiled. "It relieves my heart you could be unsure about anything, my lord." Then she lowered herself onto the sofa closest to the warm fire. She was poised on the edge of the chair, her back straight, appearing as delicate as a rose in winter. Suddenly he felt like a hulking brute.

"Fanny—"

"Sebastian—"

They laughed.

She flushed becomingly. "Please Sebastian, you speak first."

He went over to her and handed her a glass of brandy and sat next to her. She took a tiny sip, her nose wrinkling.

"I cannot say it is palatable." She met his regard unflinchingly. "What were you saying?"

"It is our wedding night."

Her fingers clutched the glass in a seemingly fierce grip. "That it is."

"I was desperate to marry you because I did not want to dally and let you slip from my grasp again. That lack of courtship makes me feel decidedly unsure how to proceed tonight." He cleared his throat, calling himself all sorts of name for what he would suggest. "Perhaps now that we are married, we should take the time to learn each other before we get to know each other carnally."

Her sweet lips froze in a small O. it took such discipline for him not to reach for her, tug her to his chest, and kiss her.

Her eyes searched his intently. "You would do this, Sebastian?"

"Yes." He was the biggest fool alive, for his damn cock was aching something fiercely.

"It seems a sensible proposition, but I do not want to wait," she whispered.

Everything in Sebastian stilled. "Are you certain?" he asked, his heart pounding.

"I have no notion of what to expect, and I fear if we wait, I will be consumed with the fevered imagining of something awful."

He couldn't help smiling. "It isn't awful. I

daresay if it was, we'd already had a revolution on our hands."

She laughed shakily. Instead of offering a reply, she leaned forward and pressed her lips to his. Need quaked through him. He allowed her tentative exploration, taking the glass from her and resting it on the carpet. Then he tugged her to him slowly, until she was seated on his thighs, thankfully away from his already bulging erection.

With a soft sigh, she deepened her kiss, slipping her hands around his neck. His wife tasted of brandy, strawberries, and heaven. Yes, he was certain there was nothing more divine than her flavor. He lifted his hand to her face, gently cupping her jaw, angling her for a more intimate kiss. Fanny relaxed, her lips parting, her tongue sliding against his. He groaned. She sighed. And their kiss burned.

He kissed her repeatedly, sometimes ravishing, and other times savoring her sweet taste. She grew restless, sliding down his thighs until her delightfully rounded buttocks pressed into his cock. His wife stiffened momentarily, before sinking into the heat of their embrace.

He lowered one of his hands to her knee, tugging the nightgown up to her thighs. Sebastian almost smiled when she released his shoulder to push his hand away. He changed tactic, ignoring the wet heat he wanted to explore for now. Instead, he drifted his hands up to her slender throat, his strokes slow and arousing. He pulled the collar of her nightgown low and slipped his finger below the hem of her chemise. His body swelled, hardened, every muscle taut, hot, aching. It was the hardest thing he had ever done, restraining himself when his body cried out to tumble her quick and hard.

She jerked, and he ruthlessly made his kiss wetter, deeper, and with a whimper, she surrendered, arching into his embrace. The tip of his finger touched her hardened nipple, and she squeaked into his kiss, pulling away. Her eyes were heavy-lidded with arousal, her lips red and swollen, her cheeks flushed.

Holding her aroused gaze, Sebastian pulled down her nightgown and chemise to her waist, baring her firm yet heavy breasts to his ravenous eyes. Her entire body blushed pink, and he could see that she fought not to hide her charms. He placed a hand on the small of her back and arched her to him. Her eyes widened, and she bit her lower lip.

Sebastian sucked a ripe berry nipple into his mouth. She screamed and pushed from his lap, stumbling into the sofa, yanking her nightgown over her quivering breast.

"Did I hurt you?" he asked gruffly.

She looked fevered and a little shaken. A silence filled the music room, and she swallowed hard, keeping her gaze averted. With a soft curse, he pushed away and moved toward the door, annoyed with his lack of control.

"No don't go I...I was just startled that is all, you may continue," she said primly, but there was a sheen of tears in the eyes she stared at him with in bewilderment.

He went over to her and stooped, so she looked down into his face. "Listen to me, Fanny. I was not considering your sensibilities. I mean you are a *lady*, and I am a great brute. We will wait and—"

A thoroughly horrified expression filled her eyes. "Sebastian," she said with surprising firmness. "I am not a child. I am your *wife*. It was simply unexpected. I...perhaps if we go to your chambers and...and turn out the candles, I would be more comfortable in the dark."

Genteel ladies should be loved in the dark where we protect their sensibilities and delicacy.

That long-ago admonition from Percy swirled through his mind. The refusal hovered on his lips for Sebastian was truly unable to imagine being so repressed with his wife. He'd always been a man of strong appetites, and he wanted Fanny more than he had ever craved anything in his entire life. What she asked was so simple, yet so frightfully complicated. What if she never became comfortable with him? He hungered for his wife in the most lurid fashion, and she was such a genteel creature. *Perhaps she only needs time.* And he would do anything to make her comfortable, even sacrificing his own needs. "If that is your wish."

Relief lit in her warm eyes. "It is, oh thank you, Sebastian."

He stood and held out his hand which she clasped. He tugged her up and made his way from the music room down the hallway and up the stairs to his chamber to have a proper wedding night.

CHAPTER 7

Fanny's heart beat an agonizing rhythm, her sensitized skin tingled with every caress, her husband's warm, masculine scent filled her lungs. The smell of him aroused a curious sensation within her, between her legs ached most strangely and wonderfully. And his kisses…she purred into the lips that seduced her with devastating expertise.

He turned her around, pressing a hot but so soft kiss at the back of her neck. And then he started to undress her. No words had been spoken as they climbed the stairs, and no words had been uttered once they entered the chamber. He'd simple snuffed out the lamps and candles which had bathed the masculine and tastefully decorated room in a warm glow. Then he had taken her in his arms, and her entire world had caught fire at the exquisite sensations he roused in her heart.

He pressed a kiss on her bared shoulder blade, and she trembled, a blush heating her skin. Though he had taken away most of the light, that roaring fireplace danced and flickered with enough light to make her decidedly anxious. Soon her nightgown was whisked from her body, and her chemise pushed to her waist.

Fanny gripped the firm fingers on her waist. "My lord…"

"Sebastian…wife."

Oh, the possessive tenderness in his voice stirred something sweet and achy low in her stomach.

"What is it?" he asked, his breath fanning her ears.

To stand before him naked would leave her with little dignity. Fanny's throat burned, and she felt uncertain. "Must…Must I be unclothed, my lord?"

She was terribly conscious of those searing eyes upon her. The hands at her waist tugged, and she turned around into his arms, lifting her chin to meet his regard.

"I must own that it does seem shocking to a lady with your fine sensibilities, but bedding is an act typically done without clothes on," he murmured.

She bit her lips, how mortifying. "I…I…"

"You can leave on your chemise, wife."

A shock of deep awareness and recognition flashed through her. That admission cost him something. But what? Shadows danced in his eyes, and her heart trembled in reaction.

"Sebastian—"

He kissed her. Hot, deep and carnal. With a sigh she parted her lips to his questing tongue, returning his kiss with ardor.

The room shifted, and with a muffled gasp she gripped his shoulder, delighted with the ease with which he lifted her into his arms. A few steps later, he placed her in the center of the large four poster bed, putting them in welcomed darkness.

She lay there, nervous and expectant while he climbed off, and divested himself of his clothes. The room was dim, and shadows were deep, but there was enough illumination from the fireplace, and Fanny could not look away as her husband slowly revealed himself to be the finest specimen she'd ever seen. A flash of golden muscle, a hint of shadows here, powerful thighs, and then he was back on the bed, blanketing her with his body.

Dear God. It was about to happen. Fanny felt faint. A desperate feeling of unreality crept through her. He braced above her on his elbows and pressed the softest of kiss to her lips and tears pricked behind her lids. Sebastian slowly deepened his embrace and the tension which had reclaimed her limbs gradually dispersed.

Without releasing her lips, he pushed her nightgown to her hips, and nudged her legs wide, cradling his weight between her open thighs. The deeper he kissed her, the more profound the ache low in her stomach became. Fanny quaked in the cage of his arms when Sebastian's wicked fingers delved between her splayed thighs, finding the hot, wet place between her legs and rubbing gently. The abrasion of a callus heightened the sensation into a fiery ache. Her breathing came harshly, and she swallowed, adjusting to the strangeness of his intimate caress.

His fingers moved over her folds, and she arched her hips toward his questing fingers. Yes. *Yes*, this was what she had wanted, but she remained silent. Ladies should not be wanton or beg their husbands to touch firmer, to rub that aching spot harder.

Their lips parted, and though her eyes were wide open in the dark, she could barely discern his features. A kiss brushed her lips, then her jaw. And dear god, he slipped a finger deep inside of her. There was a slight pinch, a brief flare of discomfort, and then Fanny felt a low, hot pressure inside. To her shame and delight, she wanted more.

He moved his finger back and forth, and she gripped his shoulders, desperate for an anchor against the storm. She could feel it building, whipping through her blood, igniting deep within her body. The sensations became too much, and she slapped a hand over her mouth to control the wild cries that wanted to spill forth. A second finger entered her. A whimper escaped, and he paused.

"Am I hurting you?"

"No," she whispered hoarsely.

"Are my fingers too callused?"

A weird embarrassment touched her. His fingers were touching her *there*. "I…I…they are fine."

"You are too tight."

Now he sounded frustrated, almost uncertain.

Mortification swallowed her, to be conversing while his fingers were in her most private of places. "Is that bad?"

A soft grunt came from him, and his touch disappeared, leaving her empty.

"I'm not a small man," he said, sounding

frustrated. "And you are small and tight. I need to prepare you more."

She had no answer for she did not know what he meant. Had she displeased him with her reaction? Oh, why hadn't she questioned Darcy more?

He shifted in the dark and pushed her legs wider. Her entire body burned with embarrassment and Fanny was so grateful he had cocooned them in the darkness of the curtained four-poster bed.

A breath of heat wafted across her mound, and then Sebastian's mouth settled between her legs. Fanny gasped, her entire body flushing with heat. He licked along the wet folds of her sex, and the pleasure that pierced low in her stomach pulled a guttural groan from deep within her. Her eyes widened in the dark. *Dear God*, what he must think of her. He licked along her sex again, and a wanton wail echoed in the chamber. "Please, stop," she sobbed, gripping his hair and yanking.

He froze. "Fanny, are you well?"

She scrambled back, pushing the nightgown down her legs. It was all too wicked.

"What you just did…it *cannot* be decent."

Darcy hadn't mentioned anything this scandalous, and Fanny was certain it was…*wrong*.

But it had felt so wonderful. A hot rush of mortification flamed through her.

"I've offended your sensibilities again."

"I…I…n-no." She closed her eyes, feeling on the verge of tears.

How could she explain to him that it all felt too intimate? Such intimacy in the marriage bed she hadn't ever imagined, and she had always hoped that she would feel some level of comfort with her husband. There was none of that between them. His presence filled her with heat and hunger and such need that bordered on painful. There was *nothing* comfortable in how he made her ache, and she hardly knew what to do with these feelings.

She cleared her throat. "I think perhaps you were correct earlier. Might…might we get to know each other a little bit first before…before we are this intimate?"

The silence was awful. *I am foolish.* "Sebastian?"

"We will wait," he murmured, shifting up to lay beside her. "There is no rush. We have a lifetime before us."

The furious pounding of her heart eased, and she did not tense when he slipped his hand around her waist and tugged her into the solid wall of his body, halting the need to flee to her chamber. He was still naked, but she didn't let it fluster her much. Clearly, no one told him lords and ladies slept in separate chambers. Could she expect any gentleman-like conduct from him?

"Sebastian, I am very sorry I——"

"There is nothing to apologize for Fanny. You are a very sheltered young lady, and I am certain I shocked you fiercely."

There was something deep and unfathomable in his tone. She turned it over in her thoughts trying to understand. "I've disappointed you."

"I am only frustrated, but it is not something to worry about. It will ease soon."

She snuggled deeper into his embrace. "There is an ache…in me…and I feel so unfulfilled I want to scream. Is that the same frustration you feel?"

She felt the smile against her hair.

"Something of the sort."

Oh. She shifted, settling atop his chest even more comfortably, distantly amazed at how secure she felt in this moment, though she was acutely conscious her husband was indeed naked.

"Perhaps——"

He squeezed her gently. "We will——"

She turned in his arms and pressed her lips to his, ending his protest. "I know my duty as your wife." His heart pounded against her fingertip resting against his chest.

"I want to give myself to you, but I cannot…" she fought the blush. "I cannot do anything as wicked and improper as you'd done earlier," she whispered, mortified at the mere memory of where he had placed his mouth. "Darcy never mentioned anything that you did earlier. She said it would be mildly pleasant…and be over quick, and you would be very mindful of my sensibilities. If we…we should remain under the covers and not be wicked, it should be all right."

There was a long contemplative silence.

"I am gathering that you will never be comfortable with me touching and tasting you so wickedly."

She gasped. "Of course not, how could you think it?"

Eventually, he let out a ragged breath. "I'm sorry," he said gruffly. "I knew ladies were not fit for bedroom romps."

Why did she feel disquiet instead of relief? Fanny hated the confusion twisting through her. His tone indicated other types of women were fashioned for the kind of loving he wanted. *Mistresses?* She stiffened, her heart pounding. Was this the reason gentlemen took other women to their bed? So as not to distress their delicate wives' dignity and sensibilities? A fierce denial surged through her heart. *It could not be.*

"Is there a particular thing you like to do?"

That soft, curious question halted her frantic thoughts. She turned and relaxed into his embrace and rested her hand atop the hand he had encircling her. An unusual warmth filled her chest, and she smiled. "I enjoy riding so very much. To feel the wind on my face, and to feel the power and strength in my mare. Riding is one of the reasons I look forward to retiring to the country at the end of the season. It is not quite the same trotting down Rotten Row."

"Do you expect to retire to the country?"

She frowned. "Only at the end of the season."

"I've never retired to the country before unless I visit my factories in Manchester, Sheffield, and Leeds."

She absently traced patterns over his knuckles with her fingertip. He had the hand of a worker, not delicate and soft like her brother's. "You keep the townhouse open during winter?

"Why would it be closed?"

He sounded so flummoxed she laughed lightly.

"You are a lord now. When Parliament is closed, and the season has ended, men of your ilk retire to their country homes for a spot of hunting and even attend several house parties. It is more relaxing there, and I daresay we get to recover from the bustle of the season."

"It is surprising lords, and ladies of society believe they need to rest from the leisure and debauchery of the season." His tone was caustic. "Men of *my* ilk work, I have thousands of workers depending on me, I fear I do not have the luxury to retire away for months after indulging in a season of dancing and other nonsense."

For several long moments, her mind became such a blank. "Of course." There had been a few rumors he made no allowances for the frivolity of society, finding it nonsensical. The chasm of difference between them suddenly loomed. Their lives had been so different and would perhaps continue to be. Fanny could not envision herself wintering in London. And clearly, he would not be in the country with her. *Perhaps with a mistress?* She bit her lower lip, frowning. What if he should turn to another for his pleasures because she had been too silly about consummating their wedding vows? It struck her then how impetuous she had been in marrying a man who operated in a world far different from hers. *And why?* Because he made her tremble? Ache with no idea of how to relieve the tension that simmered in her blood?

"I recently bought a manor in Derbyshire, Selbourne Hall. It boasts over one hundred rooms and sits on over two hundred acres. It is undergoing a few repairs, but it will be ready for occupancy within the next two weeks, I was assured."

The tight band around her chest eased, and she smiled. "Is it staffed?"

"No."

"I will begin interviewing a housekeeper and a butler. For here, we will also need more staff."

"We have a housekeeper and—"

She kissed him, and Fanny could not say who she startled more. It was absurd, but she needed to taste him, needed the feel of pleasure to push away the disquiet worming through her. She needed him to crave her and feel as if only her kiss, her touch, and her bed mattered. The hunger flaming through her was as shocking as it was fierce, and she slanted her lips over his with wanton greed, her breasts pressing hot and soft into his chest. Her husband groaned, and his heart jerked, and at one point, he trembled.

He shifted, once more placing her beneath his wonderful weight, taking control, gentling her aggression, transforming her kiss from marauding to sweet and passion filled. The softest of kisses peppered over the bridge of her nose, her lips, and down to her neck, then back up to her mouth. *Oh.* A slow heat burned through her, and soon she became lost in the wonder of his kisses. This time when he pushed her chemise to her hips and settled between her legs she did not protest. She welcomed him, feeling safe and cherished in the comfort of the darkness. A tug of longing pierced the heart of her for the illicit kisses he'd bestowed earlier, but she pushed it down, immersing herself in the way he worshiped her with gentle kisses and languid touches of his fingers. His calluses abraded her skin, rasping delightfully over her sensitized body.

His knees parted hers. The kisses went deeper, and then there was a pressure at a point between her legs where she felt empty. He pushed, and she tensed at the pain.

"Sebastian?"

"Yes, my sweet?"

"I…. Should there be pain?" Her voice was thin, shaky.

"Only the first time," he murmured. "I promise it won't hurt ever again."

Before she could stubbornly insist that it must not hurt at all, her husband's hip flexed, and his manhood surged deep inside her. Fanny screamed, her shock was so great. There was an awful burning sensation where they joined, and all the pleasure that had built from his wondrous kisses had melted.

She sobbed. "Please do not move," she whispered, fearing if he did she would be split open. Fanny could not credit women did this act, and she suspected this was why all gentlemen and society had conspired to hide this from ladies. Surely no one would agree to marriage and intimacies if they knew how painful it was.

He attempted to kiss her, and she turned her lips away from his causing his mouth to land on her cheek.

"Ah, my sweet please do not cry."

Her breath hitched at his warm tones, and this time when he kissed her, she parted her lips and allowed him in. His lips drew her pleasure forth, quickened sensations low in her stomach and took her away from the pain. For several long moments, nothing mattered, but the taste of him, and the throbbing feel of him pressed into her sheath.

"I've wanted you since I met you," he whispered in between gentle but ravenous kisses. "For two years you've haunted my sleep, and now you are my wife." His words brushed against her skin like a caress, and she craved more. Soothing murmurs spilled from him, and she delighted in his praises of how soft and delightful she felt and tasted. His weight pressed her deep into the mattress, and soon the awful burn gave way to pleasure. Then he moved.

Sweet heavens. It wasn't hurting anymore, in fact, it felt tolerably nice, perhaps more than *nice*.

The moan came from deep in her throat, and she bit her lip recalling Darcy's words that a lady must be silent during the act lest she displeased her husband. Fanny pressed her lips against his shoulder tasting his sweat, breathing in his rousing male scent.

His powerful body was moving against hers with an urgency that she responded to, and the heat quivering through her expanded and swelled. Something was building inside, and she reached for it desperately, except it blew away from her when with a deep groan her husband emptied his seed inside her.

Sebastian eased from her flesh and hopped from

the bed heading over to the basin on the washstand. He returned and gently cleaned her with a cool cloth. How she blushed and ached for there was still something needy twisting through her. There he went again, and she watched his shadow as he moved around the darkened chambers. Would he now insist they return to separate rooms. Darcy had told her that was how it was done. Only when they coupled did a lord and lady share a chamber. Instead of commanding Fanny to her room Sebastian slid into the bed and tugged the quilt over their bodies. He drew her to him and the knot of tension she had not been aware of eased.

"Are we to share chambers?"

He tensed. "I want my wife in my arms when I sleep. I've gathered that's not how the polite world does it."

His voice was rich with mild mocking amusement, but she did not mind it. In truth, his desire filled her with an inexplicable pleasure. And the last thought she had before she tumbled into the oblivion of sleep was that she quite looked forward to understanding the layers of her viscount.

CHAPTER 8

Two weeks after marrying Sebastian Rutledge, Fanny opened her eyes, greeting the warm sunny day with an unusual heaviness in her heart. She was not contented with her marriage. Perhaps it was too soon to feel so listless, but she couldn't help being aware there was an ache in her heart, and she had no notion of how to fill it. Sebastian treated her with the proper civility owed to her station. She had never boasted of a superior understanding, but to Fanny, it created a distance between them she could not breach. Each night she anticipated him coming to her bed, and her husband did not show. She would hear him moving around his great chamber and anticipation would knot up her stomach, and she would pace the floor fretfully until she climbed onto the bed exhausted and slid into a restless slumber. How absurd that his disinterest should prick her vanity, but indeed it had been wounded. Had he not found pleasure in her arms? Or was it normal for married couples to copulate so infrequently? It hadn't occurred to ask Darcy when she had been imparting the wisdom of intimacy.

She slid drowsily from the cozy warmth of the four-poster bed as a perfunctory knock announced her lady's maid Mary. She popped in, dipping into a quick curtsy before heading over to the armoire to select a day gown for Fanny.

The week before she had hired several members of staff for the townhouse to her husband's bemusement. In addition to the housekeeper and the cook, they had a butler, two footmen, two chambermaids, and Fanny had hired the housekeeper's daughter who had been in training as a lady's maid at a baronet's house. The first day Sebastian's housekeeper had referred to him as Lord Shaw with evident pride had flummoxed him. Fanny had only smiled, sensing the pride they took in working for him. It also relieved her heart that she hadn't had to ask for formality. Their new butler had immediately referred to her as "Your ladyship or Lady Shaw," and everyone else had followed suit. Sebastian had flatly refused the services of a valet, but Fanny had convinced him by arguing that he would be robbing a young man of gainful employment who would otherwise be unemployed. She'd taken pride in that victory for she had accurately read the benevolence of her husband.

"Is the viscount gone for the day, Mary?"

Bright hazel eyes glanced around. "Yes, my lady. Before the crack of dawn, mum said."

Each morning she would venture into the breakfast room to learn her husband had already headed to work. The very first morning the notion had startled her. Fanny wasn't used to living with men who worked and found herself wondering what her husband's days entailed. What did he do? What should she do? Before marriage, her life had been about preparing for the season to encourage a courtship. Then when Lord Trent had made his intentions known, the days had been filled with talking long walks, leisurely picnics where he had read poems to her, and in the nights at balls, they had danced. She hadn't done anything since her marriage but hiring staff and improving upon the dinner menu. Before Sebastian had eaten very simple fares, and while Fanny had advised the cook to keep the dishes he especially liked, she had added a few of her favorite dishes, and some puddings, cremes, and jellies. She had responded to several letters and invitations which Darcy had forwarded her and even had a couple of callers the day before. Her frustration had seen her accepting invitations to six balls, and two musicales, only now she was uncertain if her husband would be her escort recalling he had no use for such frivolity.

Fanny couldn't envision what to do with tomorrow, next week, or the other days to follow. Surely it could not be the quiet days she had been spending inside. If that were so, she would become afflicted with ennui, a state she feared she was already experiencing.

"Mary, please have Williams inform the mews I'll be taking the carriage out. And have the cook prepare a picnic basket and ensure there is a bottle of wine."

Almost an hour later, Fanny, garbed in her most sensible dress—one of pale yellow muslin with a cinched waist and close-fitting bodice trimmed with white lace, matching hat perched atop her curls—and half boots, descended the carriage which she'd ordered to take her to her husband's offices. She had been unflinching in her demands, and despite the coachman's initial hesitation, he hadn't balked in transporting her to this part of London. There was a most peculiar odor wafting on the gentle breeze—smoke, rotten fruit, and possibly the Thames.

Fanny stepped down into a dirty, narrow cobbled stone street, acutely conscious of the noise and the crowd. A few questionable gazes settled on her, mostly well-dressed tradesmen's wives. None appeared as elegantly dressed like her, and Fanny felt decidedly out of place and more than a little uneasy. She could feel the weight of their curiosity. Was it so odd for a lady to be seen in these parts? Even the flower seller who had been pushing her cart down the street stopped and peered at her. Lifting her chin, she made her way to the step of a large brick and gray wooden building. She took them, walking toward the doors with her husband's name stenciled above it.

She opened the door to a large tastefully decorated foyer. Plush dark green carpet adorned the floor, and the walls were painted in cream. The rooms leading from the foyer seemed to be made up of offices where a large number of clerks were busy, transcribing information into large account books or searching shelves for some other document. One clerk bustled past her and she enquired, "I am looking for Lord Shaw," and was directed by the bowing clerk that "the master is upstairs," before he hurried off to another room. She made her way up a neat but fairly restrained staircase to the next floor where one of the doors was labeled Sebastian Rutledge's office. Fanny entered finding a large room in which she noticed an enormous desk stood against one wall, several neat stacks of papers were placed upon it. Several chairs were strewn about with no order. Lines of shelves covered another wall, and the air was redolent with lemon wax which was a pleasant respite from the odors outside. Two men were bent over several sheaves of papers which they were discussing, oblivious to her presence. A small hallway pointed toward a single door, and she gathered that was her husband's personal office.

She delicately cleared her throat, and their heads snapped up. Immediately they jerked to their feet, evidently astonished by her presence.

"I'm Lady Shaw, and I've come to see my husband."

A short, rotund man rose from behind one of the two desks in the room and approached her. He pushed his glasses atop his nose and hurried around the large desk.

"My Lady, please excuse the mess. Let me inform Mr... Lord Shaw, you've come to call."

"There's no need," she said with a smile. "I'll announce myself. Please, gentleman return to your work."

They stared as if they were unsure what to make of a woman in their domain. Ignoring them, she made her way toward the door, faltering when raised voices reached her. She made out the cold, clipped tones of Sebastian.

"Unacceptable. And I'll not adjust my stance," her husband said in a tone which brooked no softening.

"You are treading on dangerous grounds Rutledge; the other owners won't like it. You are giving the workers ideas. If there is a strike, the blame will be laid at your door," an unknown voice snarled.

A slap echoed as if someone slammed their palm on a desk.

"Will you not change your mind, Lord Shaw?" A milder toned man asked. He sounded a bit deferential, certainly more respectful than the first voice Fanny heard.

She lifted her knuckle and rapped on the door.

There was a pause, and then Sebastian said, "Our meeting is over, gentlemen."

Footfalls sounded, and the door was wrenched open, and she peered into the astonished face of her husband. He glanced behind her, a black scowl settling across his features.

"Did you come alone?"

Oh. Her pulse tripped, and a blush spread across her face at the soft reprimand in his voice.

"Fanny?" he demanded at her silence.

"A footman rode atop the carriage with the coachman." She cleared her throat aware of his incredulity and lifted the basket the cook had prepared. "I've not seen you much this past week, and I thought we might enjoy a light repast."

She smiled with serenity at his business partners. "Gentlemen. I seem to have interrupted a crucial meeting."

Silence lingered, then a faint smile touched Sebastian's lips, and pleasure glowed warm and rich in his eyes. "It would afford me much pleasure to do so, Fanny."

She glanced behind him at the two men who stared at her with palpable curiosity. Her husband made no effort to introduce Fanny when he drew her inside his spacious and well-situated office. Their lips tightened, and they exited without glancing in her direction.

"I suppose there is a reason for your rudeness?" she asked, curious as to what their argument had been about.

Sebastian grunted softly but made no further reply. It was a spacious office, and she sensed he was a man who did not like to be confined. For his office was the size of their drawing room at home, or perhaps larger. It was not cluttered either. A large desk dominated the room, but there was a bank of curtained windows overlooking the street and river, a large Chinese painted screen blocked some direct light from the windows. It was cozily warm as the fireplace blazed merrily, a small coffee table, and a comfortable sofa which invited repose, together with several comfortable chairs.

Her feet sank into plush Aubusson carpet as she made her way to the sofa and lowered herself onto it. He sat beside her, and his stare as he watched her unload the food was a physical caress.

She quite liked the way he stared as if riveted by her. *But why have you been avoiding me?* And suddenly she knew she had struck the truth. He was not at all comfortable with their marriage either, but it flummoxed her why he hadn't made some sort of attempt to find comfortable grounds. He was a man so self-assured and powerful. She couldn't imagine he would shy away from getting close to her.

Unless...

She glanced at him. "Are you by chance in love with another, my lord?"

"I beg your pardon?"

She tilted her head back to look him in the eyes. "You heard me."

He seemed bemused. "No...you are the only woman ever to capture my regard, Fanny,"

Delight shivered through her. She felt hot and achy and wonderful from that soft assurance. Flustered she withdrew the plates, delicately arranging a few edibles for their consumption. She handed him a plate.

"Thank you," he murmured.

They ate in silence for a few minutes, and she hated how awkward it felt. She sneaked several glances his way, each time to find him chewing thoughtfully while he watched her. Fanny searched for a topic of conversation, a bit annoyed that he did not start some discourse.

"Your meeting earlier seemed unpleasant?" she asked, dabbing at her lips with a napkin.

A ghost of a smile touched his lips. "The other factory owners are not particularly pleased with me."

"May I inquire why?" Fanny hoped he did not sprout some nonsense about it being an affair for men.

Her husband placed his half-eaten plate onto the small table and hauled himself to his feet walking over to the bank of windows. "There isn't any one reason," he said gruffly. "It is complicated."

The breadth across his shoulders seemed tense, and though he stood with his hands thrust into his pocket, she could sense the tension thrumming through him. She too lowered her plate, rose, and walked over to him. Fanny stood close enough so they touched, and she leaned her head against his shoulder. He jolted slightly but did not pull away. She had no notion why she did it.

"Perhaps there is some way I could help?"

He did not dismiss her offer.

"Look at them," he murmured.

She lowered her gaze to the bustling street filled with detritus which men, women, and children skirted around, with a purpose in their steps. A street urchin stole an orange from a cart, and a flower seller leaned against a grimy brick building looking wary. This was a part of London she had never seen before, and she could not identify with the society below. But her husband did, and it was that awareness which prompted her to ask,

"What do you see?"

"People. The force that makes our city thrive, they are the working men, women, and children, men like me make our profits from. They are hard workers, filled with pride and a determination not to be swallowed by the metropolis. I pay my workers better rates than all the other factories, and recently I hired several doctors to look after the health of my employees in my various foundries. That saw dozens of other workers, mostly the women leaving the other factories and coming to me for work. The smoke and the pollution are hard on their lungs, and they deserve proper care. I've also ordered the construction of new housing in Manchester and Sheffield, made with better materials and with good sewage disposal. None of the other owners appreciate my forward thinking."

How astonishing. "And that is resented?"

"It is."

"I should think the other owners would model their work ethics from yours, not complain about it," she said pragmatically. "And it is also a kindness that is needed."

"Those cheap, greedy damn bastards only care about the money lining their pockets."

She said nothing at his profanity, feeling a sense of pride that he would be so natural with her. They stood there for long minutes as he spoke about his work and how foolish it was to hire the workers flocking to his factories when he'd already bought the machinery that would make them obsolete. It struck her how kind he was, for she couldn't imagine anyone of her society sacrificing for others.

"What will you do? Let them go?"

"No. There is a general fear that would lead to rioting. People are desperate for work to provide food for their families. While it is smart and will be more profitable to fire hundreds of workers and install smelting machines, it is also unconscionable."

A pang went through her heart. These were never things she had had to worry about, how to put food on her table or how she would provide for her children. She rested a hand on her stomach, genuinely unable to imagine such a life. She peered at the flower seller with new eyes, wondering how many mouths she had to feed, and wondering what had placed that hopeless look on her face. "I've heard that you are a business genius," she murmured, peering up at him. "Maybe you could invest in something new or start another business that would put these workers to use."

He smiled. "I already have my team working on it. And Percy has helped with positions for several women I've had to let go recently."

If she recalled his friend Percy Taylor owned several hotels, in London, and across the continent. "Perhaps you could also provide some severance package? Colin recently let go of a servant who had been in our household for years. He generously provided the man with a cottage, and enough money to live comfortably. You could do something similar for each worker you need to let go." She warmed to the idea, her thoughts buzzing. "Perhaps you could go through their employment file, and base it on their years of service and position, and pay them enough money so their families will not starve or suffer until they find another position."

He shifted to face her, admiration, and something sweeter piercing the gray shadows of his eyes. "Yes," he murmured, cupping her cheek.

His touch was firm yet light and her body hummed with nerves and anticipation. Was he going to kiss her? His regard was delightfully warm and intense.

"This is an argument I presented to the other owners to their outrage. We hire hundreds of people. That will see profits cut drastically. My proposition did not amuse them."

"You'll not back down, will you?"

His face was suddenly proud and unyielding and a bit too ruthless for comfort. "Never."

"And will you be in any danger for it?"

He was silent for long moments. "Perhaps I would have been before I was a viscount. I've learned it is not so easy to murder a peer. And if they were foolish enough to try, I can more than protect myself, at the cost of their lives if necessary."

The cold logic of his statement made her shudder. "Sebastian!" To speak so casually of killing.

His fingertip stroked along her chin lightly. Her awareness contracted to that single touch. How was it possible to be so *aware* of him?

"I have another meeting soon, wife. Thank you for luncheon. I will escort you to the carriage."

She nodded mutely, wishing to spend more time with him, liking that he shared so willingly with her as if he found her equal in wit and intelligence. "Have you been avoiding my bed?"

Fanny couldn't say who the question appalled more. Their gazes collided. Shadows, doubts, and amusement danced in his, but he remained silent.

"Are you not to answer?"

He lowered his hands from her cheek, and she was bereft of warmth. He moved away from the windows and sat on the edge of his desk, his legs splayed with insolent grace. "Your forthrightness surprised me."

She made her way to stand before him, acutely conscious of the hem of her dress brushing his boot. "And that is not an answer."

His lips smiled, but his eyes remained watchful and a bit chilled. "I can enjoy your company without bedding you, wife."

"How odd. Because we've only had dinner a few times in fourteen days, and we've made no social rounds together."

"It seems I may have been doing you a disservice, my lady."

"So, you have been avoiding my bed?"

His head dipped once in a brief nod.

She drew a hitching breath. "Why?" she demanded bluntly.

"I had the notion exercising marital obligations more than once a month would be a distressing strain on your nerves." His tone held a bit of self-mockery and some other indefinable emotion.

Still, she scowled in affront. "I am not a delicate ninny. And I would like to believe the way you made me feel extended to more than marital obligations, my lord," she whispered.

"Are you saying, wife, you feel a need for me to be in your bed?"

Fanny blushed but refused to look away from his penetrating stare. "Even if we...we do not share intimacy, it was beyond lovely to sleep in your arms," she said wistfully, recalling how empty, and cold, and lonely the silence of her bedchamber had been for the past several nights.

"Then it would be my pleasure to be in your bed, every night, Fanny." There was a carnal threat in his voice that spoke to wicked deeds and not just sleeping. The hot memory of his lips licking her womanly flesh cut through her, and it took an enormous will to battle her mortification.

She failed abysmally from the amusement that lit in his eyes.

"How breathtakingly lovely, and sweet you appear."

Her pulse jumped in her throat when he reached for her. Fanny willingly went into his arms, to stand between his open thighs, lifting her gaze to his. She swallowed when he lightly brushed his mouth across hers, slowly savoring.

"You need to go," he said hoarsely as if he were in pain.

Not yet. "Why? I am enjoying your kisses," she said shyly.

His breath exited in an audible rush. "The very taste of you is shattering every discipline I've ever used to govern my passions. I am tempted to splay you on my desk and make love to you."

"But it is daytime."

A huff of sound, which seemed suspiciously like laughter came from him.

A flush of desire swept along his cheekbones. "We can have carnal relations at any time."

The soft words burned into her heating her body with chaotic hunger. It was as he placed a fingertip under her chin and lifted her gaze to his, Fanny realized she had been staring at his chest. They stared at each other silently, a question in his gaze, one she feared she understood but hardly knew how to respond.

Brazenly she lifted her arms and wrapped them

around his back very tightly. It was all the invitation he needed to ravish her lips with deep kisses. Fanny parted her lips, moaning at the hot stroke of his tongue, and the warmth that filled her veins. How quickly he spun her senses and had hunger clawing to burst free. If she were still the same fanciful creature she had been several weeks ago, she would have fallen in love with her husband right then. *It's just passion.* Somehow, he shifted them, and now she was the one sitting on his desk, her legs scandalously splayed, her husband between them.

Good heavens!

Sebastian slowly stroked upward to her hip. She felt exposed and terribly vulnerable but wanted more of his embrace. "How wickedly wanton you must think me," she moaned breathlessly.

"I find you delightful, Fanny."

Then another soft kiss feathered over her lips. And she sighed, loving his gentleness. His wicked fingers continue their path, the pad of his thumb was rough and warm; evoking such desperate need in her blood, she shivered.

Then he was there, at her sex, and her eyes flew open. Her husband was staring at her flushed face, capturing every nuance of her passion filled expression. She was exceedingly embarrassed. "Sebastian—"

He slid a finger deep inside her. That hard but wonderful sensual stroke robbed her of breath, and she stared at him helplessly. How indecent of them, with his outer office bustling with activities only a few paces away. As if he knew her thoughts, the devil smiled at her and dipped his head, so his breath feathered across her lips. "You must be very quiet."

Her eyes widened.

Then he pulled back his finger and plunged them back into her clenching sex. Fanny fisted his jacket tightly, at the pleasure that punched deep in her stomach.

"I love how wet you get for me," he murmured, kissing the tip of her ear. His lips dipped to touch the spot below her ear.

She buried her hot face against his chest, softly moaning when he added another finger. Thankfully there was no pain, only a slight pinch as her flesh adjusted to the tender invasion. He stroked her over and over, until hunger clawed through her, fighting to break free. The piercing sensation became so much, she bit into his chest, muffling the moans she was unable to suppress. He groaned, and nudged her legs wider, pushing his fingers diabolically deep.

Fanny bucked, released his clothes and flesh from her teeth and glanced up. His eyes raged with need and lust and tender emotions as he loved her with his fingers. She trembled as if fevered, and then the tight, exquisite feeling broke, and pulse after pulse of pleasure stormed through her. *How utterly glorious.* He kissed her ravenously as she writhed against his touch, drinking her cries, and caging her into the strong comfort of his arms.

He pulled from her and tugged her dress back down over her thighs. She was uncomfortably aware of the wetness between her legs, and how wickedly they had behaved.

Sebastian stepped away. "Are you well?"

Fanny sighed, feeling languid in the aftermath of such startling but wonderful pleasure. "Yes."

"I will summon the carriage."

She nodded wordlessly, her eyes widening at the visible bulge at the front of his trousers. A desire lingered within her to please him, but she could not bring herself to make love with him in his office! She relaxed when she realized he would not offend her modesty by asking or seducing her to it, which he could have done for she had been witless just now.

He opened the door and relayed orders for the carriage to be readied. Fanny lifted her chin and met his gaze when he turned around. His expression was a tight grimace of need and discomfort, and she marveled at his restraint. "I will see you at dinner," she murmured.

There was the slightest of hesitation, then he said, "I have a prior engagement."

"Of course," she said politely, pinning the hair he had tumbled. "I'm to attend Lady Wembley's ball tomorrow evening. I know you dislike such frivolities, but will you attend with me if you've no prior engagement?"

"You seem to be laboring under a grievous misapprehension. Anything you wish of me, Fanny, I will gladly oblige. You are my wife."

Pleasure burst inside her, like the heat of the sun after a cold winter. "Thank you, Sebastian, I have also accepted invitations to several balls for the season. I'm sure we will be the butt of much speculations."

"I'm not the sort of man to be afraid of rumors."

Relief filled her. "I would appreciate breaking fast with you on occasion."

He smiled. "Done."

Settling her hat atop her head, she gathered the small basket and made her way from his office, conscious of his stare.

"Fanny?"

She paused, her hand on the doorknob, and glanced back warily.

"My previous engagement was a dinner affair at my friend's house. Percy Taylor. There will be others. Actors and actresses, lawyers, artisans, and even a few rising stars in politics, not the general lot you socialize with. Would you like to attend with me and meet my friends?"

He had offered a bridge, and a lump formed in her throat for it was a connection to a world she had never explored, and one no doubt her family would be appalled to know of. For so long her life had been about learning how to become a lady. It finally dawned that being married to this man, she would have to dismiss some of the lessons taught by her mother and governess. Fanny wasn't sure if she should be appalled or fascinated. "I would love it, Sebastian," she said unable to stop the brilliant smile curving her lips. "Thank you for asking."

"Thank you for accepting."

He seemed bemused as if he had anticipated her refusal, and she quite enjoyed that she had surprised him. Fanny sailed through the door, feeling hopeful, and astonishingly breathless. Footfalls behind her alerted her to her husband's presence. She remained silent as he escorted her down the steps and toward the carriage. Fanny paused at the flower seller, shocking the woman by offering her a ten-pound note for the entire cart with orders to deliver them to the hospital. Sebastian assisted her into the carriage and ordered the coachman to take her home and never return her to this part of the city. She gasped in outrage, but the equipage rumbled away before she could rebuke his high handiness.

Fanny smiled. He made her feel more in a couple of weeks than the marquess had made her feel in months of courting. This was a second chance to fall in love, and she did not want to shy away from it. In truth, that would be very silly when she was already married to Sebastian. Their union was permanent, and she felt the sweetest longings stirring in her heart for his touches, his smiles, and she would embrace them.

CHAPTER 9

Several hours later, Sebastian leaned against the window overlooking the gardens of Percy Taylor's drawing room in Portman Square, watching his wife indulging in a rousing, raucous game of charades. Fanny was the most delightful creature in the room, and he couldn't stop staring at her. She wore a turquoise gown trimmed with gold embroidery and delicate golden slippers, and her hair was upswept high on her head with ringlets caressing her shoulders. A few times Percy arched a mocking brow, as many would consider his female companions to be of the demi-monde. Selina, a fair-haired beauty with a willowy frame, was an actress, and Josephine, dark-haired, and petite, with a large, vivacious personality was a

French opera singer. Both women had excellent qualities but would not be considered acceptable to be in society. They seemed delighted and amused by his regard for his viscountess. His other two friends, Richard Plymouth, a country gentleman of no small means, and Theodore Dunn, a solicitor seemed equally bemused by his enchantment with his wife.

Though Sebastian lectured himself severely on staring at her, several times she caught him in the act, blushed prettily and then glanced away. Her reaction seemed to delight his friends even further. And as Sebastian had expected, they all liked her. He knew there had been some anxiety to meet her, and yet he had not doubted her reaction to mingling with people from a class she was not accustomed. Their dinner had been simple with only a few courses, but Fanny hadn't displayed any airs or discomfort. She had been all charm and genuine grace, and the tension had vanished before it had even formed.

Now she hopped on one leg and spun in a full arc, and for the life of him, he couldn't deduce what she pantomimed. Selina and Josephine were laughing without any decorum, and Richard scrubbed a hand over his face in evident bafflement.

"She's not what I expected," Percy murmured, pushing a glass of brandy into Sebastian's hand.

"Isn't she?" Sebastian asked, frowning when his wife now started to hop on two feet. For God sakes, what was she acting?

She stopped, laughing, her cheeks red with her merriment. Had he ever seen her so relaxed and happy at the balls he'd spied her at over the season?

"Yes. I thought she would have been stiff and proper and...and less enamored of you."

That got his attention and Percy smirked.

"You think her enamored of me?"

"I daresay she sneaks more glances at you and stares just as stupidly. Several times I thought to grant permission to use my guest chambers to burn off the passion simmering in the air, but I did not want to mortify her sensibilities with my ribald humor."

Sebastian sent his friend a black frown. Laughter pealed from Josephine, and they glanced toward the center of the room. She was holding onto her side and laughing with such vigor her shoulders shook, and his wife fisted her hand atop her hip scowling.

"Did no one guess an owl?"

Theodore shook his head slowly. "An owl? Why in God's name were you hopping?"

Selina joined in with the laughter and Fanny grinned sheepishly.

Sebastian smiled.

Percy sipped his brandy. "Dare I believe your uncouth upbringing finds no disfavor with your Viscountess?"

"I've seen no evidence of it." *Except we've only made love once, and it had been in the dark.* But he was coming to see it was perhaps natural shyness on her part and not a disgust of him and his baser urges. Or at least he fervently prayed it wasn't so. Today in his office, her passion had flowed over his fingers and perfumed the air. She had been a beautiful flame, whipping desire over his skin, and had almost pushed him to take her in his office. Sweet mercy, how impossible it had almost been to restrain himself.

"I believe we should play some music," Josephine said.

Fanny clapped her hands. "How marvelous. Sebastian is simply wonderous at the piano. You must play for us," she said hurrying over to him.

His friends stared at him astonished.

"Good God man, you play?" Richard asked,

rising from where he had been seated on the sofa by the fire. "And we had no notion of this."

His wife's beautiful eyes widened.

"I have some skills." His mother had taught him, and he had developed a love for it.

At the heckling of his friends, he moved over to the grand piano and lifted the lid. And he played, acutely conscious of his wife by his shoulders, her scent rousing his senses, and the entire evening taking him away from the woe of business and the mess he would have to sort in the following week in calming both his workers and the other owners. Many of the factory owners felt it would be like the Luddite riots all over again, so hated was the idea of machinery replacing jobs. Sebastian didn't believe it would be that severe, but he could take no chances, but for tonight, he removed all those concerns until the morning and played for his wife.

For it was for her, and only her he played. Then she started singing. Fanny's voice was warm and rich and...sultry. The harmonious blend of their skills had the room behind him hushed. They complimented each other in so many ways, if only it extended to the bedchamber. Her passions were buried beneath years of propriety lessons. Sebastian acknowledged then he was falling deeply for her and he needed to start peeling away all her layers more, for he did not want to be a damn fool in love while she barely tolerated him.

A COUPLE OF HOURS LATER, Sebastian and Fanny strolled along the fashionable Grosvenor Street, and his viscountess seemed quite delighted with life. And Sebastian was pleased. She was a beguiling complexity he hungered to unravel. So shy and sweetly innocent but she held her own tonight like a queen at court. They had enticed her to be brazen, and she had challenged his friends to be genteel. Her voice as she sang held them enraptured and Selina had stared at his wife with such hunger and envy Sebastian had feel for his friend who struggled for the limelight on the stage. Fanny would steal every show and conquer the heart of every gentleman if she had been a showgirl and Selina had seen it.

Somewhere in their journey home, Sebastian had impulsively rapped the carriage roof and alighted. Now they sauntered breathing in the crisp night air. Carriages lined the streets, and up ahead, gaiety spilled from one of the townhouses.

"Tonight has been delightful. I think your

friends liked me, well I certainly enjoyed their pleasant company."

"They loved you."

She shot him a brilliant smile which dazzled his senses. "I do hope so." A small frown marred her face. "It struck me tonight I have not met any of your family, Sebastian."

There was censure and something hesitant in her tone.

"Is there a reason for this?"

"I have only my mother."

Her eyes widened. "No cousins or uncles?"

"None that I know of."

"It is inconceivable. I sometimes lose sight of my many cousins and aunts and uncles. Your mother is eager to meet me?"

"I confess she is unaware of our marriage."

His wife faltered and spun to face him, her eyes full with incredulity and a flash of hurt. She fisted a hand on her hip. "I demand an explanation, husband."

"Mamma is taking a tour of the continent. The last letter I received from her she was in Venice or was it, Florence? She's been touring for several weeks now. It made no sense for me to send her a letter for she is constantly moving."

His wife worried at her bottom lip. "Do you think she will like me?"

"I promise you she will adore you."

An elegant brow lifted. "How can you be so certain."

"You are a lady."

Fanny considered that for long seconds. "Gentility is important to her?"

He hesitated before tugging her close to his side, encouraging them to walk to the gaiety in the distance. His hand turned beneath her touch, his fingers threading through hers.

"Very much so. She will be very pleased a fine lady such as yourself is my wife."

"I would want her to like me for my opinions and character."

"That will eventually come," he said drolly.

A carriage rumbled past them, as Sebastian ensured she was safely on the inside.

"When my father met my mother, he was a traveling merchant, and she was the daughter of a country gentleman in Cornwall. As my mother tells it, Papa tricked her into believing he was respectable and it was after they were compromised the truth of his situation and lack of respectability was revealed. As my father tells it, he fell in love with my mother at first sight, and nothing would have prevented him from marrying her. To protect my mother's reputation, her father forced a marriage. My mother has never quite forgiven my father."

"How were they compromised?"

"They were found in bed."

Fanny gasped. "I daresay there is nothing to forgive. They got in that bed together," she said tartly.

"My mother was unable to forgive my father for being so common," Sebastian murmured. "He looks like me you see. Tall and brutish with muscles more suited to working-class men and not refined gentlemen."

Her fingers tightened on his, and once again she paused to peer up at him.

"You have the most wonderful physique and your muscles, they are...are simply...they are beautiful."

"Oh? You've seen them in the darkness? Tell me more," he drawled teasingly.

His wife blushed and glanced away. "Your mother must have loved your father to be found...with him like *that*."

Sebastian grinned at her prim tone, and they resumed walking.

"I daresay she did, but I hardly saw any love between them while I grew. My father died when I was eighteen away at Cambridge. He did love her, and when I returned I observed no grief. I think she was relieved."

"How horrid! Surely it couldn't have been so?"

"Perhaps I did not fully perceive the nature of their marriage," he murmured, recalling the quiet moments in which he would spy his mother staring at his father's picture, her face a study in heartbreak and regret. "Do you regret marrying me, Fanny?"

They stopped near a lamp post, the soft light spilling across her lovely face. Her eyes were wide and uncertain. "What an odd question. I haven't had cause to reflect with regret, only a wish we...we would be closer. We've been married two weeks, and I feel like I do not know you." A becoming flush covered her cheeks. "Well except outside of carnal relations."

He tucked a wisp of curl behind her ear. "And you want to know more do you?"

"Oh yes. Our marriage is forever you know."

Forever. His heart jolted. His mouth had gone dry; he paused to clear his throat. It was then

Sebastian realized on some fundamental level, he'd expect her to slip from his fingers one day. "I'm an open book," he murmured.

She tapped her chin thoughtfully, a gleam in her eyes, one he quite liked. "You are very accomplished for one so young."

Pride swelled within his chest at her tones of admiration. That he hadn't expected. *I've much to learn about you wife.* "I worked hard for it. I never expected the viscountcy, I never even met my predecessor so removed I was from a life of elegancies."

The notion didn't seem to repulse her. He kissed her. Just a brief touch of his lips to hers, but that small touch made his insides heated. He stepped back and smiled. His wife shivered, despite the warm summer night.

"Are you cold?"

"No."

Ah...it was desire then.

"Are you in love with Lord Trent?"

"Who?" she asked vaguely, staring at Sebastian's lips, and stepping closer.

Savage satisfaction filled him that she wasn't pining away for the bounder. "The man you were to marry a few weeks ago." He hated reminding her, but several times he had found himself wondering in the nights he spent alone if she was craving the marquess.

Her eyes widened. "Oh dear."

He scowled. She smiled.

"I am not, and I think that makes me a terrible person for I had been set to marry him until I saw him with his lover. I liked him, admired his humor even and his gentleman-like qualities, but never did he make my heart race from a stare, or made my lips tingle or my stomach ache with the need to be kissed. You do that to me, Sebastian."

How easily she shattered his world. The hand he lifted to cup her cheek trembled, shocking him at the strange intensity of the emotion coursing through his veins.

"Would you like children?" she asked shyly, peering up at him with sweet anticipation.

He gazed at her, briefly at a loss for words. For so long he had wanted her because he had found her charming and attractive. Her kindness had been even more appealing than her prettiness. Many times, he had observed how she danced with the gentlemen, the bucks society ignored, and she conversed at length with the ladies no one deigned to notice. What a fool the marquess had been to let her slip from his grasp, but Sebastian was still glad the man had been an ass, or she would have been lost to him. Though he had wanted her with every emotion in his soul, he hadn't thought of a life beyond having her. But now...he could see them, in the country, strolling by the lake, and her swollen with his child, her eyes radiant with happiness. Hunger for that very picture clawed through him "I would," he said gruffly. "Like to have children."

A burning need to feel her in his arms took hold of him. "Would you like to dance?"

"In the streets?"

"At the ball."

She glanced up at the townhouse at the top of the road and then back at him. "We are to appear without invitation?"

"Yes."

Her eyes sparkled with uncertainty, wickedness, and temptation. "How naughty of us!"

A slow smile stretched across her face. And he saw her intrigue. "Be daring with me, Fanny," he teased, tugging her toward the townhouse.

Laughingly she came with him, her eyes sparkling with mischief and tender sentiments. And he wondered if her fierce vow that night when she had accepted his proposal about not wanting love held true. His heart jerked hard and then settled. Sebastian wanted her love, for she was a woman he could cherish until breath left his body. She belonged by his side and without question in his heart. How fortunate she had consented to be his wife. And he must be careful now with how wicked he tempted her to be. While he wanted to encourage the part of her which had defied the expectations of society and her family and ran from the altar, he did not want to repel her with his rough manners and actions.

Now she seemed thrilled by his daring.

They slipped inside the crushed ballroom by entering through the side gardens and hurrying up the stairs to the open terrace windows. His wife giggled the entire time, her excitement at being so improper evident, and a joy to witness. They spilled inside the crush ballroom, and with a sigh of breathless anticipation, she flowed into his arms as the strains of another waltz played.

She moved with the grace of an enchantress, and the vigor she danced with mildly surprised him.

"People are staring," she whispered grinning.

And they were, and his viscountess did not seem to mind the least bit.

"I believe this is your first outing since you ran from the altar, my sweet. You are notorious."

She laughed, and the blissful sound traveled, and he could already imagine what the scandal sheet would report as he danced the night away with his love.

How ravishing Lady Shaw appeared at last night's ball the headlines would shout. Or some nonsense of the double jilt securing the iron king and how besotted he seemed and how enchanting his wife was. Sebastian did not care, determined to attend any ball she wished and dance the night away with her. For he couldn't imagine a better place than being in her arms like this, feeling her energy, witnessing her joy, and just being with her.

I am falling for you, Fanny...I am falling hard.

CHAPTER 10

A few hours later, Fanny was wrapped in the arms of her husband in his chamber, moaning as he kissed her senseless. They had tumbled into bed shortly after returning from the ball, and instead of sleeping as she had expected, he had taken her into his arms and proceeded to make love with her.

"Does this mean you'll be coming to my bed more than once a month?" she demanded breathlessly against his lips.

"If you would allow it, I'll come every night."

Pleasure arrowed through her. "*Every* night? Surely that isn't possible?"

His fingers stroked her jaw, over to her

collarbone, down to the underside of her breast. Her nipples ached, and it hovered on her lips to ask for his touch there. A delicate tendril of heat spun through her body.

"Let me put on the candles tonight," he coaxed pressing soft kisses to her lips and cheek.

"I...I..." Anxiety seared her. "Perhaps the next time." Her throat went tight, and she so hated to disappoint him.

He made no reply, only kissing her with passion. She fisted her fingers through the thick strands of his hair, and melded her mouth to his, responding greedily. Sebastian stumbled with her to the bed, pressing her down and crawling over her with his powerful form. He glided his fingers over her sex in a heated sensual stroke before he had positioned and pushed his thick length deep within her.

Now he rocked slowly, but deeply into her snug channel. She tried to hold onto her dignity as he spread warm kisses to her neck and below. A sharp tug on her nightgown bared her breasts, a hot breath fanned over her nipples, and she stiffened. He paused and waited until she relaxed.

"Do you trust me, my sweet?"

"Yes." Her voice was a mere whisper.

"I cannot see you, so let me touch you...kiss you. It won't hurt, I promise it."

He pulled down her nightgown even farther and took one of her nipples into his mouth. A cry tore from her, and she bucked in his arms. Then he started rocking again, and she grew wetter and wetter.

"I love how you bathe my cock with your passion, Fanny," he murmured roughly, his pace increasing ever so slightly.

She blushed grateful for the dark. She had no notion what cock meant, but from the dark lust vibrating in his voice, she knew it to be wicked. *I like being wicked.* Acting on carnal instinct, she lifted her legs around his hips. Her husband groaned his approval, and though his smooth movements remained controlled, each thrust pierced deeper. She could feel the heat in her body, the sweat on her skin, and would not want him to witness her wanton reaction, yet in the same breath, she desperately wanted to see his face. Did he have that desperate mien of lust as he'd had earlier in his office? That wildness in his gaze, the sensual slant of his lips?

He kissed her, burning away all her musings.

She clutched at his shoulders. His muscles twisted under her fingertips and the knowledge he was naked roused her to a fevered pitch, and she felt herself hurtling toward that bliss she had felt earlier when he'd loved her with his fingers. With a soft scream, she shattered, and a few thrusts later her husband joined her.

Her breath came in shuddering gasps, and it took a few seconds before she regained her composure. Sebastian pressed a kiss to her brow and gently disengaged their bodies. He pushed from the bed and parted the heavy canopied curtains which had cocooned them in darkness. As it were, the light from the fireplace barely outlined his shape as he padded to the small table and returned with a washcloth and pressed it between her legs.

After ensuring they were both tidied, he drew her into his arms so that her head pillowed on his chest.

"I received word earlier today that the minor repairs are completed on our country home. Should you wish to journey down soon, let me know."

Fanny smiled. "And will your businesses not suffer?"

He grunted softly. "I am hiring a few more stewards and managers."

She twisted to face him and peered up into his face. "To what purpose did you hire them?"

"So that I can visit my office only twice per week. I want to spend more time with you wife."

Impulsively she hugged him, and he chuckled. Drawing back, she lifted her fingers and traced the curve of his lips. He was smiling, and suddenly she felt silly that she insisted on darkness when they made love.

"And you will retire with me to Derbyshire?"

"At least for a week or so, I'll be there with you. I am quite looking forward racing you."

"How surprised you will be when I trounce you," she murmured sleepily, snuggling into his arms, quite glad she had trusted in her instincts to visit his office earlier.

ANOTHER FEW WEEKS PASSED, and Fanny's admiration and affections for her husband grew. In truth, she was quite certain she was falling in love with the man. A notion which would have frightened her a few weeks previously for she did not like heartache or her expectations to be disappointed. But there was nothing more permanent than marriage, and she had given herself leave to bask in the glorious delight she felt in being with her husband daily. Though Sebastian did not like it, she visited him at his office, of course with no less than two footmen accompanying her, and had lunch with him several times.

"Is that all, your ladyship?" Mrs. Campbell asked, and Fanny got the sense the housekeeper had requested an answer a few times.

She grinned, scandalized with how often she spent thinking of her husband. With a smile, she handed the housekeeper the changes she had made to the menu for next week and the list of items she required for a dinner party she was planning next Friday evening.

"Yes, it is, thank you, Mrs. Campbell."

She smiled and dipped into a quick curtsy before bustling away.

Fanny then made her way to the room her husband used as a personal exercise room. The door was slightly ajar, and she pushed it open wider, her breath hitching at her husband's state of undress. She didn't usually venture into his domain, but he had requested her presence several minutes ago. Unable to help herself she greedily ran her gaze over the graceful but powerful lines of his body. Muscles corded Sebastian's shoulders and back, and they twisted with each dip and roll of his shoulders. He was tall, lean, and so handsome, a dart of heat arrowed through her. Her breath quickened, and a rush of pleasure filled her heart by merely looking at him. Was this why he craved to see her naked?

She stepped into the room and closed the door.

He faltered and grabbed a towel from the small sofa to his left and raked it across his skin. His chest was an expanse of beautiful golden skin, chiseled with muscle. How desperately she wanted to touch. As if he read her mind he grinned, carnal invitation firing in his eyes. She scowled, for her husband would probably attempt to seduce her as he tried yesterday in his library before dinner. Fanny feared she wasn't adventurous enough to indulge in those kinds of debauchery, and it fretted her at times. Sebastian seemed so virile and insatiable, making love with her often. While he came to her bed every night, she could feel the tempered restraint in his touch, and the battle he waged with himself. Last night, he had bit out a curse of frustration and had pulled from her, parted the curtains, and lit a taper casting light into his chamber.

He hadn't wanted to make love in the dark anymore, and Fanny had hardly known what to do with herself. It had been too unexpected, and she had been unprepared. Her husband had stared at her for several moments, then closed his eyes, and apologized for frightening her. She hadn't been frightened really, merely startled. When he had made to out the candle, she had gripped his hand and tugged him down to her. Fanny hadn't the courage to remove her nightgown, but they had made love with that single light. She had been able to see the flash of raw hunger in his face, the piercing need in his eyes, the sensual slant of his lips as he had ridden her longer and a bit harder than she had experienced before. How wonderful it had been. Except he had seemed so tense afterward as if he waited for her recrimination. They had remained silent until she had fallen into deep slumber.

"You asked to see me, Sebastian?"

"I did," he said, walking over to cup her cheek and press a kiss to her lips. "I missed you." Another kiss, and with a pleased sigh, she parted her lips for a more intimate embrace.

"And also, because we must speak about this need you have to visit me in the office. I do not like it."

Fanny stepped back with a frown. "I thought you enjoyed my help immensely?"

"I do, but yesterday's incident has left me unsettled, wife."

"Oh, Sebastian. I only had a few coins in my reticule, and the boy did return it after he learned that he robbed your wife."

Her husband scowled, seemingly unmoved by her argument.For the last several days she had been assisting him at his office on Whapping Street. She would take lunch, and after dining, she assisted him by sorting through the records of the employees, he would have to terminate in the coming weeks and write a suggestion on a severance package, and artfully worded recommendation letters.

The first time she had suggested a severance payment of two hundred pounds for a man who had worked in his factory for ten years. The lawyer in the room had spluttered his outrage and suggested as a woman she had no notion of business matters for the two hundred pounds was far too much when they had to fire hundreds of workers. She had tartly responded as a woman she had the heart and compassion he lacked and had offered the bulk of her inheritance to Sebastian's astonishment.

She had almost choked when Sebastian revealed the magnitude of his wealth and that he could afford to pay everyone he would have to let go whatever she thought they deserved for their years of service. Her husband had fired the lawyer immediately to her distress, but she had convinced Sebastian to give the young lawyer another chance. They had worked together splendidly since then, and her generous severance payments were not frowned at. She had believed her husband enjoyed her presence and her assistance.

Sebastian prowled over to the sofa and picked up a few articles of clothing. He held them out, and beyond curious, she made her way over and collected them.

"What are these?"

He shot her a devilish smile, his eyes twinkling. "Breeches and a shirt. These are what you will wear when I teach you how to box."

"I beg your pardon?"

His head dipped, and he kissed the bridge of her nose. "You heard me, my sweet. You and I will be dancing on this mat at least twice a week. That way I will rest better knowing if you are ever accosted you can defend yourself."

Her husband had the oddest notions. "You would like to show me how to defend myself?"

"Yes."

Fanny felt bemused. "I will not be taking lessons with you," she said primly, hurrying to replace the clothes onto the armchair of the sofa.

Provoking amusement lit in his eyes. "Then you will not be revisiting that side of town wife. I have the time for a lesson now if you are free."

"Sebastian!"

He arched a brow toward the breeches and shirt. With a huff, she grabbed them up, thoroughly scandalized. His amusement deepened as she tossed him a glare.

"I do hope you realize how outrageous this all is."

"Is that the reason you are fairly bouncing with excitement?"

She grinned for she was genuinely delighted. "I shall be back shortly."

"You could dress here," he murmured. "I will happily play your maid."

A shock of desire shivered deliciously through her body at that improper suggestion. They stared at each other, and the dare in his gaze robbed her of breath.

"Undress for me, Fanny."

Her husband circled her as if she were prey. His warmth pressed into her back, and she felt the proof of his arousal. "Is it to be a lesson in boxing or one of ravishment?"

His laughter was soft and hot against her neck. "There will come a day my sweet where I'll have you splayed, naked on that sofa there and I will feast on you."

Fanny whirled around, clutching the clothes to her chest. Sebastian's eyes were watchful and curious, and she got the sense he had been testing her. She spluttered, unable to credit acting in the lascivious manner he suggested. Unable to proffer a reply, she hurried from the room, her face flushed and her heart racing, and her husband staring at her with amusement and something far more troubling that she was unable to identify.

With the aid of her lady's maid, she changed into the scandalous garments and returned to his domain. Almost an hour later, Fanny sprawled indecorously atop the mat in the room, utterly exhausted, and uncertain if she wanted to still make an afternoon call on Darcy whom she hadn't seen since her marriage. They had corresponded through letters, and Fanny had thought it quite odd, that she hadn't seen Darcy and Colin at the few balls Fanny had attended with Sebastian.

"I wanted to have a small dinner party next week," she said winded, still working to settle her breathing. The rudimentary motions of thrust and skip away he'd shown her had seemed so simple until one repeated the motion over and over with a husband who seemed more machine than man. "Then I am thinking to host a ball toward the end of the season."

Her husband, the dratted man, lay beside her, his breathing unruffled. "Whatever you wish, Fanny."

"I would like to invite Josephine, Selina, Percy, and Richard and Theodore to dinner and the ball."

Sebastian turned his head on the mat, and their gazes collided. "You know they aren't normally invited to society events."

"I know," she murmured. "I enjoy their company immensely, and they aren't disreputable in the least. If you approve, I would love to extend the invitation."

His lips curved. "I'm certain they will be thrilled, but society will be offended."

"I never knew you set stock with other people's opinions."

"I don't."

"Then I daresay as your viscountess I should have your mettle," she teased. It had startled Fanny that the few balls they'd attended people had seemed welcoming. Her genuine friends hadn't cared that several scandal sheets branded her *the double jilt*, and those who had appeared inclined to frown upon it had forgiven the incidents relatively quickly. She'd soon realized it was her husband's wealth they coveted after the several hints that were discreetly delivered to her.

He chuckled, and she heard the warm approval in it. "Then it is settled," Sebastian said. "Invite whomever you please to our table and house. And I must also tell you, wife. You are an apt pupil, very quick and graceful."

Warmth burst inside her chest, and she grinned, suddenly glad she had indulged his odd notions. Acting with playful instincts, she shifted and rolled atop of him, settling her bottom atop his lower stomach. Sebastian sucked in a harsh breath, his muscles clenching beneath her, and Fanny grinned. How she loved surprising him.

"I am of a mind to ravish you," she murmured, biting gently on his chin.

"Ah, my sweet, such wicked words are music to my ears."

Fanny smiled at his hopeful look. "You remind me of the cocker spaniel I had as a child. He was always so hopeful I would feed him treats and he softened me up with a similar look!"

"*Woof.*"

She laughed. "You my lord are outrageous."

"But you like it."

"I love everything about you," she said softly and then stilled at what she implied.

He searched her eyes. "Fanny?"

Her heart pounded, and she stared at him helplessly. *I love you*. She could not say the words. When did it happen? And how could she be so certain? It was just ridiculous to perceive the beautiful way he made her feel, the pleasure that would swarm through her from a simple kiss was love. They'd only been married a little over a month.

"Fanny, I've lov——"

She kissed him passionately and with a furious need burning inside her to stop the words she feared he might say. It was impossible to describe the feelings cascading through her at the realization he could have a tendre for her as well. Only a few could ever hope their marriages would have more than warm affection to sustain its lifetime. Their tongues tangled, and the sweetest of heat burned through her body for him. *Is it joy or trepidation I feel?* Speaking their growing sentiments aloud would make it seem so much more real, and if it was real, then it could be snatched away. She needed longer to savor the idea of love before she could own to the feelings he aroused in her heart.

She pulled away. He grinned, and her stomach flipped. Why was he so appealing?

He brushed his fingertips along the curve of her throat. "I lov—"

Again, she silenced him with a kiss, and this repeated whenever they broke apart, and he tried to say the words until they dissolved into fits of laughter.

"Oh, I see," he murmured, his lips wet with her kisses, his arousal a hard brand beneath her buttocks, his eyes burning powerful with emotions that made her insides hot and achy. "I see, indeed, my viscountess."

She could barely breathe, let alone speak. Fanny blushed, what did he believe he perceived? That she was suddenly and inexplicably afraid to want his love and have it ripped from her, like all her previous attempts? That the revelations flowering through her were more intense and real than anything she had ever felt? She was falling in love with this man. With him, Fanny felt comfortable, desired, cherished. Pushing away from him, she lurched to her feet, feeling the weight of his stare as she rushed from the room as if the devil was on her heels.

CHAPTER 11

The next day, Fanny descended the carriage with the aid of the footman at her former home in Mayfair. She hoped Darcy was at home and had not taken herself off to the country. The letters Fanny had sent around yesterday had received no reply from her friend and she was concerned. She decided to extend the invitation to dinner in person and find out if her friend was well.

She marched up the small steps, and the door opened before she could knock.

"Jeffers," she said warmly greeting her former butler.

His weathered faced creased into a smile and be bowed. "Lady Shaw, how wonderful to see you again if I may say so."

"Oh, you may," she said with a laugh, handing him her light coat, and removing her bonnet. "Is Lady Banberry home?"

"Her ladyship is in the drawing room. She'd asked not to be disturbed earlier. If you wait in the smaller parlor, I will announce—"

"There's no need. I will knock and announce myself." With that, Fanny made her way down the hallway and knocked on the drawing room door once and then opened it. "Oh Darcy, I've missed—"

Fanny gaped at the sight of Darcy and Colin locked in a passionate embrace. They were only kissing, but Darcy had always been such a stickler for propriety the scene was shocking. Fanny spun around when her brother hauled his wife even closer, and with a groan cupped her buttocks.

She closed the door, ensuring it slammed. A gasp sounded and then a muttered curse.

"Fanny?" came Darcy's startled cry.

"I did not mean to intrude on your privacy," she said blushing. "I never thought you would be… kissing." In daylight, and in such an intimate fashion. Certainly not after the speech Darcy had given Fanny on how a lady should conduct herself with private matters. She had been happy for her friend's guidance, even though lately she had been yearning to touch and kiss Sebastian on more than his lips.

A lady must never be wanton in her desires.

You'll repulse your husband if you show yourself to be too eager for the marriage bed.

You must lie silent and not be vocal in your responses. It will be perceived as vulgar and unladylike.

Those were a few of Darcy's instructions she remembered with clarity for they were some of the hardest to adhere to once Sebastian took her in his arms. She turned around to see her brother and his countess respectably composed. He made his way over to her and hugged her.

"It is good to see you, Fanny, I trust you will stay with us for dinner?"

Her noncommittal response was muffled against his chest, and she returned his embrace fiercely. "Is mother back from Bath?"

"She's opened the house at Camden Place and intends to stay for the entire season."

"I've been married six weeks and mamma is still prostrate with disappointment? It isn't likely to change," she said with amused exasperation.

"You know mother. She will come around when she is of a mind to recall that Viscount Shaw is three times wealthier than the marquess."

Fanny scowled at her brother who ignored it and bestowed a tender smile toward Darcy then departed. Fanny made her way over to the sofa, sat, and settled comfortably against the cushions. Darcy pulled the bell for tea and cakes. She peered at Fanny, an unusual glow in her eyes. It was perhaps one of happiness, and Fanny was heartened to see it.

"I see things with Colin have improved?" Fanny probed delicately.

Her friend blushed. "I daresay it has. I packed my trunks and was about to depart and he begged me to stay. Oh Fanny, it has been glorious since," she gasped, clutching her rosy cheeks.

Fanny grinned. "I am happy for you. When you did not reply to my note yesterday I dreaded the worst, that you were so unhappy you were abed."

"Nothing of the sorts, we...I...was just busy." She blushed so prettily, she gave Fanny an inkling just what activity had kept her friend busy.

A maid entered with a tea trolley, and they waited until she arranged the tray on the small satinwood table, then departed. Darcy poured the teas and handed Fanny a cup.

"Are you content with the viscount?" Darcy asked skeptically as if such a thing was improbable.

Fanny laughed, and her friend's eyes widened. "Oh yes, I am. I am exploring and learning and loving. I am happy." And the knowledge settled deep inside. If only she would be brave enough to explore the wild desires thrumming inside of her, and to strip away the restraint she could feel in her husband's touch when he loved her. "Dare I ask why you are glowing?"

"Oh, Fanny, I cannot tell you!"

They stared at each other, and then laughed.

"Are you truly happy, Darcy? Has Colin stopped...whatever he was doing?"

Darcy sipped her tea as if gathering her thoughts. "You are married now so I will speak frankly. I was going to leave him, and I cared not one whit about scandal."

Fanny straightened from her casual repose. "Leave my brother?"

"Yes. He had a mistress, and he visited her once a week even though he came to my bed every night," Darcy said hoarsely, a flash of pain blanketed her face before she gathered her composure.

Anger and disgust surged through Fanny. "Why would Colin dishonor you and the vows made before God. I know he loves you."

Darcy blushed.

"What is it?"

"It is not fit for your ears," Darcy said primly, even though her hazel eyes danced with amusement.

"Don't tell me this is another secret that must only be known by men of our world, how utterly silly and outrageous."

Darcy sighed and gave a little apologetic smile. "There are things men need that a lady cannot do. Collin did not want to dishonor me, and he felt honor bound not to disgust my sensibilities."

Fanny could only stare at her. "What utter rubbish!"

Darcy grimaced. "My mother told me gentlemen would always have their mistresses and it is the way of the world, but I believed Colin was beyond such temptations. He loves me, I love him and that should have been enough. I gave him an ear full. To both our amazement I slapped his face. I was so distraught."

"But you've forgiven him?"

"We've reached a compromise," she said.

Fanny stared at her, her mouth going dry. "What sort?"

"Fanny I cannot say!"

"Darcy do not be silly, we are married women and you are my dearest friend, you can trust this particular confidence with me."

Darcy looked away. "These are things only fast and immoral women would do but it seems my husband craves these acts." She didn't seem disgusted at the notion more fascinated and her face was scarlet.

A flash of knowledge tore through Fanny. Darcy had done these very acts she wanted hidden. *Oh.* She sat awkwardly, her heart beating wildly. "Is...is one of these things making love with your husband fully unclothed...and not in the dark?"

They were both blushing by the time her question ended, and Darcy giggled. "Fanny, this conversation is most improper, but *yes.*"

Then she changed the conversation to the mundane, and Fanny listened half-heartedly speculating what else Sebastian required of her that only loose and immoral women would normally do. And wondering why she was so terribly fascinated? And frightened...and breathless...and curious.

A COUPLE of hours after visiting Darcy, Fanny returned home. She'd responded to a few letters, mostly charities soliciting her patronage which she gladly provided, but thoughts of the desires her husband might be keeping from her had overwhelmed her, distracting her from the tasks at hand. With a sigh, she pushed aside the packet of letters and lowered the quill onto her writing desk. Fanny stood and exited the smaller drawing room which she had commandeered as her personal space. She made her way to the room in which her husband practiced his boxing, and the voices floating through the door alerted her that he was not alone. Percy Taylor had come to call again, the third day in succession if she was not mistaken.

"You should take a lover…that is what you need if you cannot go to your genteel wife for your needs."

Shock froze the greeting on Fanny's tongue. Though the door to the exercise room was ajar, both men's backs were to her and seemed engrossed in their conversation.

"Don't be ridiculous," Sebastian snapped, scrubbing a hand over his face. "I am not discontented."

He shifted from his friend, his side profile stark

and uncompromising. Her heart trembled and the uncertainty swamping her senses was unbearable.

Percy jabbed at him, and her husband bounced away, his feet shuffling with grace and speed as they danced around each other in a rhythm that was now familiar to her.

"Come man, do you take me for a fool? The last time you demanded we spar every day was when you had hoped to work away your frustration because of how badly you wanted Lady Fanny and she was beyond your reach. Now you've married her and weeks after here we are pounding away again. You are not happy with her."

She jerked and pressed a hand to her chest, silently urging them to see her hovering in the doorway. The will to step away was beyond her grasp, yet a part of her did not want to hear a confession where the man she was falling in love with found her lacking. Then Percy Taylor glanced up and their gazes collided. Fanny wanted to wilt with relief. This sordid conversation would now end. Instead, his lips twisted in regret and his lips parted.

He said, "You will have to procure a mistress so as not to upset your viscountess's sensibilities. You know it is the sensible thing to do man, or you'll drive yourself crazy from frustration."

She hated him violently at that moment for even suggesting something so vile. He stared at her unapologetically. Her throat ached, and her eyes burned. Fanny shifted her regard to her husband who still had no notion she waited by the doorway; her breathing suspended for his answer. He made no reply, tipping his head to the ceiling and pinching the bridge of his nose.

A bleak pain twisted through Fanny's soul at the look of pure hunger that settled on her husband's face.

"I do need more from Fanny. I am not at all certain it will ever happen. But I knew she was a genteel soul when I offered for her, so I must adjust my expectations. I am content."

Even to her his words sounded hollow. She pressed trembling fingers to her lips.

"So, will you take a mistress then?" Percy asked ruthlessly, still pinning her with his golden gaze. "If your lady wife cannot satisfy your urges you know that is what you must do."

A mix of emotions assaulted her senses—pain, rage, denial, and loss. The husband she had been falling desperately in love with wanted another woman, for Fanny did not please him. She feared her chest would split wide open to show her crushed heart. Foolishly, she had hurtled herself impetuously into such intense feelings for him, and he found her wanting, and hadn't even had the decency to speak with her about it, as married couples should.

"No," came Sebastian's flat and dismissive reply. "I would never dishonor Fanny so. I must simply suppress any desire that will likely repulse her. I couldn't bear if she were to view me in the same manner my mother saw my father."

Except his words of affirmation to their union were not a balm. She felt wretched, and she must have made some sound for his head snapped up, and he stiffened when he spied her, every line in his body going rigid. Fanny whirled around and hurried away, ignoring his calls. Was this how Darcy had felt? *Dear God.* How humiliating to think she did not satisfy his hunger, especially when he made her so happy and her soul content. However, what she lacked would drive him to another, and she would never forgive such a betrayal.

"Fanny!"

Grabbing the skirts of her dress, she lifted them and ran away, bounding up the stairs to her room. His footsteps echoed against the parquet floor as he raced after her. She shoved into her chamber, trying to close the door before he came in on her. Sebastian pushed through the door and she slowly backed away.

"Get out, my lord."

"No." He wore only a trouser and was bare-chested and bare feet. He advanced as she backed away. "Let me explain, Fanny what—"

"I heard enough," she said, her breath itching on a sob.

"You heard nothing but the foolish utterances of a misguided friend offering advice that was unwarranted. I would never betray you."

"I saw your face!"

He faltered.

"You craved. You needed more...and it was not me who you thought of."

His jaw visibly flexed. "It was you," he snapped, a fierce storm brewing in his eyes. "Every lascivious thought and image that crowed my damn mind when Percy spoke was of *you*, us. You have been interred in my mind and heart for over two years. I assure you, wife, no one can replace you. I met you at a ball two years and three months past and you did not notice me. But you were imprinted in my heart, your smile, the sweet way you laughed, the habit you have of tucking your hair behind your ear when you are nervous. In the months I waited in agony that you would deign to notice me, I've never had a lover. You have been my only lover since I saw you, and it offends me that you believe so little of my character you think I would ever dishonor our vows."

Thick, fierce tension swirled around them.

"And you thought so little of my character you never thought to speak with me about the things you find lacking," she said hoarsely.

He flinched. "You are a lady, *Fanny*, I...I...I am rough in my ways and coarse in my needs." A rough groan of frustration issued from him. "And we are giving it more weight than it needs. I was not born a lord with genteel ways, but I am not a goddamn animal. I can control my needs."

Something inside her seemed to break, crumbling to pieces, and dissipate. "I find nothing repulsive about you," she said. "I cannot perceive you would believe it. I do not care that you were not bred into refinement, I quite admire that your hard work and dedication procured your wealth." She closed her eyes. "The fact a mistress was suggested to you...." She blushed, and she hated her reaction. "You discounted that discontent, but you cannot. It will break you down and make you miserable. And it hurt deep down here." She pressed a hand above her racing heart. "That I do not make you happy, as for how you've made me."

He was before her in two strides, cupping her cheeks, tilting her face to his. "Do not be foolish. You made me the happiest man when you consented to be my wife, and you've not disappointed me once. The need for more I have is sexual, and I promise you that can be ignored and never be brought up again."

Liar. She knew what dissatisfaction with her lot in life felt like, and how it could rob one of sleep and happiness. "Our marriage is forever," she whispered. "Do not dismiss the things you desire because of the misguided belief that as I am a lady, I will collapse from mortification. I need to be able to trust in your honesty with me always, Sebastian. If you honor me as you claim...I need to see all of you so that I can love *all* of you."

He hesitated a long moment before replying, "I do not want to make love with you in the silent hush of darkness with curtains drawn."

She smiled tremulously. "I can do that."

"There's more," he said, curious heat shifting in his eyes.

"Yes?"

"I want you to give me the opportunity to make love to you unreservedly. If you do not enjoy it, I promise I will respect your choice and nothing you say or do can ever diminish the regard I have for you, Fanny."

"Tell me," she breathed.

"I want to see all of you. I want to love you in the nights and the days. I want to spread you wide and lick all over. I want to be sweet and gentle, but I can also be rough and demanding."

Fanny's heart beat a too fast tempo. She licked her lips, and he slid his thumb over her bottom lip.

"I want these lips to suck my cock with tight pulls."

She stared at him, confused, mortified, and then the full image unfurled in her mind. *Oh God*. A shock of heat tore through her and between her legs ached. She pulled away from him and pushed a loose wisp of hair behind her ear.

He smiled tenderly. "There is no need to be nervous."

"And you'll not think me vulgar?"

Anger fired in his eyes. "A woman's passion is never vulgar. It is honest and beautiful, what society calls wanton, I call sensual. Whoever has told you that nonsense deserves a bullet."

"And what you did that first night...when you placed your mouth on me *there*, you'll want to do that?"

The hunger that flamed in his eyes had her stepping away from him warily. She found herself holding her breath. He made no advances and she slowly relaxed.

"Let's take a walk in the gardens, sit outside and read. We need not speak of this anymore," he said softly.

"I am dusty from travel. I will take a bath and meet you within the hour?"

He nodded, and her throat ached at seeing wariness in his eyes. He left her room, closing the door gently. An odd sense of shock tore through her and an awareness flowered. He truly believed her refined sensibilities would never allow her to be the sensual creature he craves.

Fanny collapsed onto her bed, hugging a cushion to her chest, fighting against the ache pressing against her heart. How little they still knew each other, even though she could feel the admiration he had for her. He wanted to make love with the light...and he wanted her mouth on him.

To stand before her husband naked seemed beyond shameless and allowing him such awful intimacy was incomprehensible. The giggle that slipped from her was startling. It hadn't occurred to Fanny that people cavorted so and found pleasure in it. Clearly ladies did not, and their men found mistresses to alleviate their sexual desires. Well, that was what Darcy alluded to earlier and Fanny thought it an outrageous excuse to dishonor vows made before God. She sensed the honesty in her husband when he said he would never dishonor their vows. He'd wanted her for over two years and he had waited.

She smiled, falling in love with him completely at that moment.

CHAPTER 12

Sebastian felt stuck on the uncertainty and pain he'd seen in his wife's eyes. How could she doubt his affections? *Because you've been keeping a part of yourself from her.* And now she felt as if he did not want her. What rubbish, with every breath in his body he ached for her, and not just to make love. Her gentle smiles had a way of making him feel seven feet tall. She was witty and compassionate and so damn sweet she made his teeth ache. She made his day brighter when she visited the office, and her dedication to helping him with his work without much care that it would be frowned upon by society filled him with admiration.

You craved....

The memory of her hoarse pain filled voice raked at him.

But it is for you I crave my sweet. And he would spend every day showing her that, and not the way she would expect. He desired her beyond sexual pleasures. Sebastian did hunger to be free with his urges with her, but he wanted her to see he loved *her* and not how damn good she made him feel between the sheets. They had a lifetime together, and he would slowly remove all the shyness and eventually love her in the wild and untamed desire she roused in him. He would be honest with her in every regard.

"Forgive me if I overstepped," Percy said stiffly, from behind him.

"Why are you still here?" Sebastian had slugged him in the gut when he'd come back down from his wife's room. He'd left him doubled over in the library, entirely uncaring, for he'd realized Percy would have known Fanny was standing there and had deliberately injured her with his thoughtless remarks. Percy was now dressed but still looked a little green in his face.

"It took me a while to recover," came the wry reply. "I am truly sorry. I thought...I thought I was helping, but I should not have interfered. Will I see you at tomorrow's dinner?"

"I'll be taking my wife to Derbyshire this weekend. I never gave her a honeymoon." How silly of him. "I believe we'll be doing a spot of traveling. Paris and Vienna, I think."

There was a long pause. "Don't hide any side of yourself from her," Percy said. "For so long you thought you were foolish to want a lady so far above us...you in everything. But I can see that she loves you, and you are just as captivated by her. I will apologize to Fanny most sincerely when I next see her and let her know I never meant it and that I only wanted to prod you both to act. I will see myself out."

Sebastian made no reply, and the soft footfall of his friend retreated. He poured another brandy in his glass and sat down upon a comfortable chair that had been set at the side of the room. He sipped his brandy, rolling the liquor around in his mouth to fully appreciate its quality. He had a lot to think about.Fanny had never told him she loved him. *I love everything about you* was not what he wanted from her.He wanted so much more. He smiled, recalling how she had silenced his declaration with passionate kisses. She hadn't been ready to hear those words, and he found he wanted to hear them from her, quite desperately.

A rueful smile curved his lips, he was never the desperate sort. But in this too he would be patient. A knock sounded, and he turned around.

"Enter."

His wife's lady main bobbed a quick curtsy. "Lady Shaw has asked for you to attend her my lord?"

"Thank you, Mary," he said finishing his brandy, before setting it down with a decisive *clink* atop his desk. He made from the library, down the hallway, and up the stairs. He knocked on her door once, opened it, strolled inside, and faltered. His wife was not in her chamber. He glanced at the connecting door.

Then the soft smell of lavender floated on the air, and he knew his wife was behind him.He turned, and just like that he'd forgotten how to breathe. There his wife stood, evidently fresh from a bath, dressed in a flimsy dark blue silk banyan which clung alluringly to her damp curves, her glorious mane of blonde hair tumbling to her hips in wild disarray. She was a beguiling clash of innocence and provocative temptation.

Heat pulsated along his cock. "Fanny, I thought

we were going for a ride," he suggested hoarsely, for if he gave in to her at this point, he would surely send her running back to her Mayfair family home.

She took a deep, steady breath, then reached behind her, and twisted the key in the door, shutting them in. The key went into the pocket of her banyan. His heart roared because she was committed to her evident intention, and he had to rein in the dark lust that rushed through him. He sat on the edge of her bed, splayed his legs outward, silently willing her to come to him. Though he wanted to grab her into his arms and kiss her senseless for being so brave and loving, he remained seated. All of this had to be her decision, and if she changed her mind, he would understand. He'd always thought it impractical how sheltered ladies of the *ton* were kept about intimate relations, but now he understood how significant a step this was for her. Her trust and love for him humbled Sebastian, and he knew then with every part of him that she loved him as much as he adored her.

A smile lifted her lips and then she sauntered toward him, such innate sensuality in her movements his breath hitched, and blood rushed to his groin. She stepped between his splayed legs and met his gaze. Her eyes raged with such emotions, anxiety, embarrassment, and love. He gripped the edges of the mattress to prevent himself from reaching for her.

She leaned in and pressed a kiss to his lips. "I am falling in love with you, Sebastian. Please, let me rephrase. I am hopelessly in love with you."

All his warnings to himself telling him to move slowly with his wife burned away like ashes in the wind at her earnest declaration. Desire swept through him.

Her lips curved. "I love—"

He kissed her, hotly and with a will he hadn't known he possessed gentled his mouth. "You must know that you own my heart. I love you, Fanny, desperately."

Her tongue darted out to moisten her rose-tinted lips. "You will have to help me, husband, I am in unchartered territory," she teased, her breath fluttering against his lips.

He released his death grip on the edge of the bed and trailed his fingers along the line of her neck to the hollow of her shoulder. "It is daytime," he said softly.

Amusement lit in her eyes. "I know."

"I will devastate your sensibilities, my sweet. We can go slower. Light candles tonight and remove your gown. Then we will take it from there."

There was a breathless pause. Their gazes collided, and his gut tightened. His cock hardened on a surge of need so painful his hands trembled against her cheek.

"Devastate me."

❧

SEBASTIAN WATCHED her with an unreadable intensity that sucked all the air from her lungs. An almost cruel sensuality harshened his features and nerves fluttered in her stomach, taunting her earlier confidence that had seen her determined to shock his senses by seducing him. She wanted her husband to know that she could be as bold and adventurous as him, and the excitement that had burned through her veins had prompted her to act.

The very idea of being so wicked and daring, had a familiar ache settling low in her stomach. She also felt ridiculously vulnerable. Holding his gaze and willing herself not to blush, she stepped back a few paces, and shrugged the silken robe off her body, standing naked before Sebastian.

A sharp intake of breath pierced the air.

"Sebastian?"

He remained silent, his eyes devouring every dip and hollow of her body. "You are perfect," he said reverently.

Her cheeks suffused with heat. "Take me, my love." Fanny leaned into him and gently bit into his bottom lip. "I am not afraid of your passions, nor am I delicate. I am your lover, your wife, your friend. Love me until I scream your name," she whispered shyly.

With a groan, he slanted his mouth over hers fiercely as if the tether on his control had snapped. Their tongues tangled wildly, and a long, low moan broke from her lips.

"I want to lick you," he whispered against her lips, a dark flush accentuating the sensuality of his face.

She trembled as agonizing need coiled in her belly. "Then lick me," she purred, her heart beating so fast she felt faint. Fanny gasped when he lifted her into his arms and within a few strides lowered her onto the wingback chair, and with very deliberate actions splayed her legs wide, and then urged her to recline into the cushions forcing her to rise onto the tips of her toes with each foot to keep her legs wide. The position was very provocative, and her entire body flushed at the raw hunger which leaped into his eyes as he slowly perused the carnal way in which she sat in the chair.

She cleared her throat delicately and gripped each side of the padded armchair, ensuring she kept her legs widened. "Sebastian...I am in a chair, and the bed is over there."

"This is where I want you."

Fanny waited, her heart a pounding mess, anticipation skittering against her nerves as he shrugged from his shirt and trousers, dropping them carelessly onto the floor. Her eyes widened, and she stared at the masculine beauty of him. "Oh Sebastian, you are so beautiful."

Her breath hitched when he sank to his knees in front of her.

"You are a goddess who deserves worshiping, you are so beautiful and sensually formed Fanny," he murmured, his eyes devouring her. "You are blushing all over."

She wetted her lips. "We are being *very* decadent."

Her husband leaned forward, and she dipped slightly, so their mouths melded together in the softest kiss he had ever given her. It asked for trust, and it also reassured, and with a sigh, she surrendered her inhibitions. He released her mouth to press kisses against her shoulder, her chin, down to the sensitive hollow of her throat, and even further down. He flicked his tongue over a hardened nipple, before rolling it gently and sucking. The pleasure was so sharp she wailed before slapping a hand over her lips.

He released her aching nipple to peer up at her. "I want to hear every cry, Fanny. Hold back nothing."

She breathed roughly, her breasts rising and falling with her quick breathing.

One of his hands gripped the armchair right where she held on and the other...*dear God*. He glided his fingertips as he stroked over her aching sex. She was already shamelessly wet for him, and he groaned his pleasure. He shifted, lowered his mouth to her sex and licked. A wild cry tore from Fanny, and she gripped the armchair even tighter.

"I've dreamed of this," he whispered against her sensitive flesh.

His tongue teased her over and over, until something hot and powerful coiled low in her stomach. Fanny burned, sweat trickled down her breast, and she lifted her hips helplessly against his wicked mouth as he tugged her nub between his teeth and lashed it with his tongue. All her modesty vanished, and a wild delight overwhelmed her senses.

"Sebastian!" Her entire body convulsed as she splintered apart, pleasure cresting through her in waves.

He stood and swept her into his arms. They stumbled toward the bed, and he laid her down as if she were precious. She smiled, understanding just how much he cherished her. Holding her gaze, he spread her legs wide with his, fisted the length of his manhood, and breached her opening. Her body was wet, soft, and yielding and she welcomed him as he thrust deep inside of her. The impact of his penetration jarred her, and the edge of pain rode the pleasure that tore through her body.

Her hands stroked over his shoulders, his hair, the powerful muscles of his back as he loved her with deep, rough, and wonderful strokes.He whispered carnal encouragement, promising her all the different ways she would be worked onto his cock, and that she would love every moment of it. She believed him, for bliss was tearing her apart.

She took a deep, steady breath, which released on a long wail of exquisite pleasure as he rode her long and hard. Her fingers gripped blankets beneath her, her head twisting against the pillow. He lifted her legs higher across his back, causing him to sink deeper into her aching sex. Pleasure grew inside Fanny until it expanded and burst forth in white-hot bliss, cascading delight through her body. With a deep groan, he tightened his hands and emptied his release inside her still-shivering body. He gently pulled from her and wrapped her securely in his arms. They stayed like that, their breathing heavy, then laughter spilled from her.

"That was amazing, not that our times together haven't been wonderful," she said, still laughing, "I never knew. I feel I should write a book and send it to all the ladies of society. I suppose only mistresses know?" she asked softly.

"Those lords are idiots."

She grinned. "Yes, they are. I really must write that book."

"Then you will need all my knowledge," he said huskily, shifting, so she splayed atop his chest, dragging her up for another kiss.

And with shock and delight, Fanny realized he was starting the madness all over again.

EPILOGUE

Two years later...
Selbourne Manor, Derbyshire

Fanny laughed in delight as her nine-month-old son, the honorable Nathan Rutledge, gripped onto his father's finger and took another wobbly step, then another. Nathan was such an adorable cherub with wayward dark brown curls that she loved playing with. She was so proud of him. Fanny pushed up to her knees on the thick blanket on which they picnicked, a hand pressed to her chest, silently cheering him on. Pride burst into her heart when he released his father's finger and took several steps unassisted. Sebastian cheered, which startled their son who paused, then dropped down onto his backside. His angelic face scrunched into a frown, but when he perceived his parents were pleased, he bestowed upon them a toothy smile.

"How outrageous," her mother whispered, glaring at the scandal sheet as she read. "People are buying this...this...book!"

Fanny pinkened as Sebastian looked up at her and winked.

The dowager countess huffed, narrowing her eyes. "*A lady's guide to love, happiness, and pleasure?* I will certainly not be reading this bit of depravity." She slapped the papers onto the grass her eyes filled with outrage. If it were ever revealed her daughter was the author of the scandalous book that was taking society by storm she would expire from apoplexy.

"I believe I shall take a walk with my precious grandson by the lake."

"Yes, madam," Sebastian said laughing, handing over their son.

The second he was in her mother's hand, her querulous expression vanished, and a look of pure loved suffused her face. She walked away, telling him stories of a grandfather he would never meet, but would one day respect.

Fanny tipped her head to the sun valiantly peeking from behind the clouds.

"A shilling for your thoughts," Sebastian murmured, tugging her scandalously to rest against his chest so they both stared into the clouds.

"Only a shilling?"

"Greedy wench. A pound then." Then he kissed her, uncaring that her mother might see, or Darcy and Colin who strolled with their daughter in the distance.

"I'm so blissfully happy, Sebastian, I cannot believe how blessed we've been," she said with a happy sigh resting her hand on her stomach lovingly.

Her husband seemed to understand the gesture, for he stiffened, and rested a trembling hand atop hers.

"You are already with child again?"

Joy burst inside her. "Yes. Isn't it wonderful?"

They shifted onto the blanket, so they faced each other. Powerful emotions darkened his eyes. "I love you, Fanny. Each day you complete me."

"And I love you," she murmured, kissing him, and silently thanking God for her beautiful family.

❦

THANK you for reading **The Viscount and I**!

I hope you enjoyed the journey to happy ever after for Sebastian and Fanny. **REVIEWS ARE GOLD TO AUTHORS,** for they are a very important part of reaching readers, and I do hope you will consider leaving an honest review on Amazon adding to my rainbow. It does not have to be lengthy, a simple sentence or two will do. Just know that I will appreciate your efforts sincerely.

CONTINUE READING FOR A SNEAK PEEK INTO THE NEXT BOOK OF THE SERIES

❦

MISADVENTURE WITH THE DUKE

Forever Yours Series Book 4

Excerpt

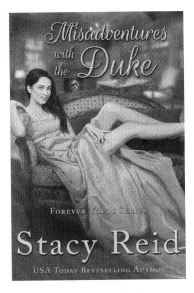

Grab a Copy Today

"A duke by any other name! Touted as honourable, and a sterling example for all young bucks to emulate, this author has it on the highest authority that a certain duke is nothing but a libertine! Grab your weekly feature to keep abreast with the Duke of Disgrace!"

Christopher Worth, the Duke of Carlyle, has a carefully cultivated reputation of 'respectability' but he possesses a dark, lustful heart which he reins in rather well. Except someone is out to reveal him as a wicked rogue in the tongue in cheek articles written about him by a notorious gossip columnist. Determined to unmask this meddler in his life, he finds his heart shockingly captivated by Miss Pippa Cavanaugh.

The hopes of marriage or the charming attractiveness of the Duke of Carlyle didn't drive Pippa to pursue the most elusive catch of the season, she was out to avenge her dear friend whose heart had been callously injured. Pippa desires to reveal to society that their perfect duke is a wicked, unprincipled seducer. The last thing she expects is for the dratted man to turn the tables on her, engaging her in a dance of wits, soul stealing kisses, and unexpected, sensual adventures. Soon she must decide if he is her path to ruin or her promise of a happy ending.

CHAPTER ONE

London, 1839

THE *HAUT monde* of London no longer whispered whenever Miss Phillipa Beatrice Cavanaugh— Pippa to friends and family— made one of her rare appearances in society. Tonight, at Lady Peregrine's midnight ball, the hushed words repeating her family's history no longer rode the air, cutting against her skin, and burrowing into her heart. Their eyes however still gleamed with speculation, judgment, and perhaps pity. As it stood only a few lords and ladies of society made overtures to welcome Pippa and her mamma, Lady Lavinia Cavanaugh, within their elevated circles despite her being the daughter of a Baron, Lord Rupert Cavanaugh.

Correction…the daughter of a disgraceful runaway Baron.

Pippa's scandal was not the typical one that haunted most society families—the reckless racing, gambling debts, a deliberate compromising, or an elopement to Gretna Green. Pippa, at only two and twenty, suffered from a tarnished reputation these last several years because of a selfish decision her father had made. The consequences had also reduced Pippa and her mother to genteel poverty. Her father's modest estate in Hertfordshire hung in limbo and disrepair, for he'd abandoned them to live with the woman he loved in America. He had written to Pippa over the years, informing her of the two children he had with his wealthy American mistress, and while Pippa's mother bitterly called them her husband's *little bastards*, a part of Pippa yearned to know her siblings.

Still, the dreadful scandal resulting from her father's decision followed them like the foulest of airs. It was as if his inconsistency and dishonor would one day show in her blood. In the five years since her father left them, the pain and disgrace of it all had seen mamma insisting they seclude themselves in the heart of the country, ignoring all invitations to town, and the indulgence of the season. Despite their steward's best effort to keep the estate solvent, they'd been informed the coffers were nigh on empty.

When her mother had wearily informed her it was time to marry, Pippa hadn't rebelled, wanting to escape the shame and pain of her papa's decision, and forge another path for herself. Perhaps there would be a new adventure within marriage, a happier life, a fresh beginning. Anything would undoubtedly be better than the tedium of country life, where she took long walks, attended church, and balls at the local assembly. The only bright spot was the romantic comedy she wrote, solely based on the life of the people in her idyllic village —Crandleforth.

In truth, the people of Crandleforth almost made their village feel like home. There, no one blamed them for her father's dishonor, and they were treated as faithful friends, family even. But Pippa still wanted to leave. Surely there was more to life than the everyday humdrum of Crandleforth and its citizens, even the pleasant ones.

Quite irritated with herself for remembering the sly, cruel murmurs that had rabidly whispered of her family's misfortune, Pippa pinned a small smile on her lips and tapped her feet ever so slightly to the dazzling and invigorating music leaping to life from the orchestras' bow. Tonight should be about the future, not wallowing in the past.

She'd been in town a week now, and the glitter and dazzle of the season had been beyond incredible. Tonight's ball was hosted in a grand ballroom at the base of a wide gold railed staircase, which allowed the viewing of all the guests entering, who were dressed in the height of fashion displaying their wealth with their elegant and elaborate jeweled accessories. Several golden chandeliers descended from the ceiling covered in a mural depicting the sky with a multitude of hues aesthetically blended together. Footmen moved through the crush bearing endless refreshments, there was laughter, chittering, and dancing. Merriment all about. This was indeed a welcomed change from the dull, yet peaceful, Crandleforth.

"Oh Pippa, I am distressed no one has asked you to dance," a hushed voice whispered to her left. "You are one of the prettiest girls here tonight! I've had six dances, and my feet are begging for relief, and you've had no requests. Why I truly cannot credit."

Lady Miranda, a dear childhood friend, stepped to her side and looped her hand through Pippa's. Her friend did not mean it unkindly, it was a simple observation. And Pippa expected Miranda's dance card to always be filled. She was slender and graceful with her golden hair piled high in a riot of fashionable curls, quite beautiful, and much coveted by the young bucks. She'd already received three offers this season. All had been rejected for the family had higher hopes for their daughter.

"I do not mind. I see no one worth the honor." And Pippa was anticipating a very particular gentleman making a sort of declaration tonight.

That was why she had been so keen on attending, despite her dismal reception at another ball three days ago, and a musicale only yesterday.

Vibrant green eyes peered down at Pippa's much shorter frame.

"Oh, I do feel so wretched, Pippa, to be having so much fun when you are only observing."

"I take joy in watching the dances, you know I have two left feet. I am sure to stomp on toes," she teased.

Miranda rolled her eyes in an unladylike fashion, which if her mother the Countess Leighton had seen, would have incited vapors and sharp corrections. It was a wonder the countess who expected perfection from her daughter, allowed her such friendship with the imperfect Pippa. Though she knew it was because of the more than decade-long friendship between the countess and her mother. Several summers as a child, Pippa had traveled to the countess's country home in Lincolnshire, and it was there the treasured friendship had grown with Miranda. Pippa was happy the countess hadn't turned away from them when the scandal had broke. She had remained mamma's true and dearest friend.

Miranda squeezed her arm. "There is a buzz

about the room that the Duke of Carlyle would be in attendance tonight, and that is quite a coup for Lady Peregrine. But I've yet to see him, and oh I do so want to!"

"Miranda do behave! And what shall you do if you see the duke?"

Pippa's friend smiled mischievously, tucking a ringlet of hair behind her ear. "Why flirt shamelessly with him, of course. I've met him previously, and I declare we would be a perfect fit! He is so dashing and handsome! Mamma would be quite pleased with me if I snagged his attention. Imagine me, a duchess! How lovely it would be."

Pippa had a particular weakness for scandal sheets, and those pages spent an inordinate amount of time on the wickedly handsome but very boring Christopher Worth, the Duke of Carlyle. A man Miranda seemed determined to set her cap at, and the only thing that seemed to recommend him to the position was his title.

Pippa wondered if she should caution her friend to be circumspect in her admiration for a man the scandal sheet lamented might never marry. It seemed he could not find a lady as tedious, exacting, and proper as himself. The tattle sheets had never reported anything remotely scandalous on the man, yet they seemed compelled to mention his very private activities weekly. Why, only last week they spoke of his visit to a circulating library. Pippa was still uncertain as to why that was newsworthy, though she guiltily admitted she had devoured the article.

Miranda craned her elegant neck, peering at someone in the crowded ballroom. "I see Lady Shelly. I must confer with her. Would you like to accompany me?"

"I dare not," Pippa said. "I am a trifle overheated and may slip onto the terrace."

Miranda nodded and made her way through the crowd, heading toward the bobbing purple turban by the refreshment table. With a sigh, Pippa glanced around, searching for the particular gentleman she had attended solely for tonight—Mr. Nigel James Williamsfield. Tonight all would be well, and everyone would see that she and her mother had recovered quite nicely from *the disaster*—the name the polite world, the newspapers, and scandal sheets had dubbed the pain that had torn through their family with such terrible, rending teeth.

Tonight, Nigel would declare for her in front of the polite world, and he would do this by just asking for Pippa's hand in a dance. How utterly simple but so complicated. Across the crowded ballroom, she met the eyes of her mother who winked and lifted her chin toward the upper levels. Pippa gasped when she spied him descending the wide staircase to the ball floor, and she had to prevent herself from pushing through the crowd to go to him. He had taken so long to reach the ball she'd doubted he would attend. Pippa laughed softly and suppressed the urge to twirl with the dizzying excitement rushing through her veins.

It was not that she sought the approval of the *ton*, but there was a deep part of her heart that wished for everyone to see that she was indeed acceptable. That the scandal did not mean that she was tainted, unlovable, or unmarriable as they had whispered for months. No gentleman required dances of her, asked her to stroll in the park or to accompany them on carriage rides. No bouquets of roses and lilies filled the hallways and parlors for her the morning after a ball. Now, a single dance with Nigel would show everyone that she was indeed marriageable and acceptable to his esteemed family despite the past scandal.

She had met him a few months past, and he had become her dearest friend for several weeks while they had taken long walks in the countryside in Crandleforth. How amiable and accepting he had been, and unflinching in his courtship when he had learned of her impoverished circumstances, and less than ideal reputation.

Her mother who had despaired of her ever securing a match had started to hope. And if Pippa were to be honest, she hadn't believed marriage a possibility for her though she had hungered for a family of her own. A husband to love, and children with whom she could share the many stories she had crafted over the years for her entertainment.

Her gaze collided with Nigel, and she couldn't help smiling widely. It had been over four weeks since they had last communicated, and Pippa had despaired that she should ever travel to London and had told him so in a letter. He'd replied, professing his love and how much he would miss her, and had lamented how droll the balls were without her presence. How thrilled he would be to see that she had managed to travel to town. They'd let their townhouse in Mayfair for the last three years to a merchant family to Mamma's embarrassment. Mamma had prevailed upon her dear friend Lady Leighton, and they currently stayed with the countess at her townhouse in Russell Square.

Her smile faltered when Nigel stared through her before glancing away. An awful sensation lodged itself in the vicinity of her heart. Surely, she was mistaken as to think he would ignore her presence. Though they hadn't spoken about it, Pippa had not been led to believe he would ignore her in a public setting.

Lifting her chin, she determined to be patient and not hasten to a conclusion. However, several minutes passed, and that heavy sensation pressing against her chest had spread to encompass her entire body. Her mother appeared stricken as Nigel passed her without acknowledging her even once. He made the rounds, and it was easy to see he was quite a popular gentleman.

It seemed so inconceivable she had been mistaken in his affection and attention. He had declared himself to her several times, and he had made it known to her mother he intended to court her. In fact, her mamma had been despondent in spirits for the last several months, and it had been Nigel's presence in their lives which had seen her rallying.

Pippa plucked a glass of champagne from a passing footman and took several indelicate sips. Oh! Relief swept through her when she espied him coming her way with his mother, Viscountess Perth. Feeling sorry she had ever doubted him, Pippa lifted her gaze to his and awaited his approach without displaying they had knowledge of each other. A soft gasp escaped her when he passed by so closely, she could have brushed the lapel of his dark evening jacket. He stopped only a few paces from her, bowed to the elegantly charming Miss Elinor Darwhimple, and requested her hand in a dance.

Pippa wanted to die from the humiliation and pain crawling through her but perversely refused to run away. Several minutes passed while she stood on the sidelines, watching her mother attempting the same feat—trying to be brave amidst a sea of confusion and dashed hopes. Pippa startled when a footman approached her and discreetly slipped her a note.

She strolled toward a column and peeked at the note.

Meet me in the conservatory. And there it was, the drawing of a rose as Nigel's signature, same as in all the letters he had ever sent her. Fury pounded through her veins, the sudden rush burning away all pain and shame she had felt. *How dare he!*

She scanned the room to see him watching her. With deliberate slowness, she tore the note into small pieces. He glanced away, bowing to the three ladies who approached him. Crumpling the little bits of papers in her hand, hating that her throat burned with unshed tears, she pushed through the crowd needing to escape for a breath of fresh air. Yet she did not hasten to the wide-open terraced doors leading out into the gardens. Instead, she made her way from the ballroom and down the surprisingly empty hallway. Pippa and Miranda had accompanied the countess on a call to Lady Peregrine for tea a couple of weeks ago, so Pippa tried to recall which door had led to the library.

Instinctively she knew being surrounded by books, she would be able to breathe, and perhaps the tight knot constricting her heart up to her throat would ease. Upon reaching the large oak door, polite habit insisted she knock, though it was quite unlikely anyone else would be in the library. When no voice called out, she eased the door open and slipped inside. The large room was awash with pale moonlight which painted half of the room in muted shades of silver and moonbeams. The embers in the large fireplace barely flickered. She strolled over to the wide-open windows, uncaring of the slight chill in the air.

The door opened, and she whirled around. She discerned the features of Nigel.

The shock had her stiffening.

"Pippa, my darling, I—"

"You followed me?"

He faltered at her sharp question. "I had to, my sweet, when I saw you tore up my note, I had to."

"You will refer to me as Miss Cavanaugh, sir, nor will you come closer," she snapped furiously when he made to advance further into the barely lit room.

He paused, and they stared at each other in tense silence. She so very badly wanted to demand he leave or slip through the windows herself to escape this confrontation. Pippa feared what his actions tonight meant, the ruination of all the dreams and hope which had been bubbling in her heart these several weeks. But she was not a coward, and she would not start acting like one now. The truth must be had, even if the pain of it broke her heart. "Why did you not seek an introduction or ask me for a dance? You pretended not to know me, as if we had no attachment."

She wasn't sure if he flinched or if it was a trick of the light.

"Pippa—"

"Miss Cavanaugh," she said, hating how husky with pain her voice sounded.

"I...I am to be married," he finally said.

She stared uncomprehendingly for several moments before accepting he meant to someone else. That could indeed be his only meaning, but she had to ask, "To someone else?"

He raked his fingers through his light brown hair, creating a mess of what had been perfectly styled. "Yes. To Elinor Darwhimple."

The shock that tore through Pippa rendered her to a marble. "It has been announced?"

"Not as yet. But we have an understanding, and the negotiations between our families are completed. The announcement will be sent to the newspapers tomorrow."

She stared at him in muted hurt and disappointment, a desperate feeling of unreality creeping through her. Finally, her lips parted, and she said, "You said you wanted to marry *me*...you even told my mother..." she swayed, the ruined dreams settling on her shoulders like a boulder. "You said you loved me and wanted to marry me."

He hurried forward to take her gloved hand in his. "And when I declared myself and asked for a kiss, you said you did not love me as yet," he reminded her with sickening earnestness as if that would excuse his offensive conduct. "You did not return my sentiments in the way I had hoped, my darling. Surely you see that I was confused by your lack of ardor and encouragement."

No...she hadn't loved him as yet, not in the way the poets described it, in the manner her mother still yearned for her father. But Pippa had liked and enjoyed all Nigel's amiable qualities, had believed in his declared affections, and had believed love...the most passionate sort would inevitably follow. She was suddenly grateful that their skin made no contact and she hadn't kissed him when he'd asked. He did not deserve such a privilege.

He had been so friendly and obliging, always seeking her company. Standing up to dance with her at the balls held at the town's assembly hall. The citizens of Crandleforth had smelled a union on the air and had even started offering congratulations long before it had occurred to Pippa an attachment was forming. Nigel had no intention of declaring for her. He had merely been amusing himself with a flirtation. Perhaps even a seduction. The *blackguard*.

The sweet, amiable way they had bantered, the laughter, the dancing, and the curricle rides had meant nothing to him. "Every word from you was a lie," she whispered. "I was honest with you, but you were only deceptive." And she had not seen through it! In the same manner, she had never seen that her father no longer loved her and mamma, and his heart had been wholly engaged elsewhere. How could she still be so naïve?

"Please do not doubt my sincerity or affections for you. I promise nothing will change, and I will still provide for you with a townhouse and a carriage with an allowance. I do not want to lose you, and you shan't lose me my sweet," he continued earnestly. "I vow it!"

Pippa felt faint. "You'll provide me with…a carriage and an allowance…." Her voice ended, and she stared at him, distress beating through her veins. She might have spent the last few years in the country, but she had enough experience of how cruel the world could be to know he referred to offering her *carte blanche*. A mistress. "You think to establish me as your soiled dove?"

"Pippa, my darling—"

She pulled her hands from his. "You are a vile, disgusting pig! And I do feel as if I've insulted all the swine in the world by comparing a man such as yourself to them."

This close she could see the flattening of his lips and the darkening of his brown eyes. A flush, evident in the meager moonlight, reddened his jawline. "Pippa—"

Her disgust threatened to choke her. "You will leave my presence immediately, or I will scream. I am certain your soon-to-be fiancée and mother will not appreciate you being discovered in a compromising situation with the likes of me."

A tic appeared in his jaw, and then he turned about and left the room. She hurried toward the door and closed it with a *snick*. A few minutes alone was required with no interruption. Her composure had to be gathered, the tears trembling on her lids suppressed before she braved the outside, and before she faced her mamma. How would she take the news?

Moving away from the door toward the window, Pippa faltered in the center of the library. A choked sob escaped her lips. How foolishly hopeful she had been. She stood there, hating the fact tears coursed down her cheeks. She pressed trembling fingers to her lips, drawing forth on the anger, preferring it to the stabbing pain in her heart. "The insufferable *pig*! That snake…blackguard…baboon!"

A low voice drawled from the darkened corner

to her left, "Come now, I am sure you can do better than that."

Pippa screamed.

WANT TO KNOW WHAT HAPPENS NEXT?

CONTINUE READING...

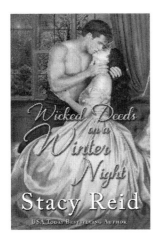

Happy reading!
Stacy Reid

ACKNOWLEDGMENTS

I thank God every day for my family, friends, and my writing. A special thank you to my husband. I love you so hard! Without your encouragement and steadfast support I would not be living my dream of being an author. You encourage me to dream and are always steadfast in your wonderful support. You read all my drafts, offer such amazing insight and encouragement. Thank you for designing my fabulous cover! Thank you for reminding me I am a warrior when I wanted to give up on so many things.

Thank you, Giselle Marks for being so wonderful and supportive always. You are a great critique partner and friend. Readers, thank you for giving me a chance and reading my book! I hope you enjoyed and would consider leaving a review. Thank you!

ABOUT STACY

USA Today Bestselling author Stacy Reid writes sensual Historical and Paranormal Romances and is the published author of over twenty books. Her debut novella The Duke's Shotgun Wedding was a 2015 HOLT Award of Merit recipient in the Romance Novella category, and her bestselling Wedded by Scandal series is recommended as Top picks at Night Owl Reviews, Fresh Fiction Reviews, and The Romance Reviews.

Stacy lives a lot in the worlds she creates and actively speaks to her characters (aloud). She has a warrior way "Never give up on dreams!" When she's not writing, Stacy spends a copious amount of time binge-watching series like The Walking Dead, Altered Carbon, Rise of the Phoenixes, Ten Miles of Peach Blossom, and playing video games with her love. She also has a weakness for ice cream and will have it as her main course.

Stacy is represented by Jill Marsal at Marsal Lyon Literary Agency.

She is always happy to hear from readers and would love to connect with you via my Website, Facebook, and Twitter. To be the first to hear about her new releases, get cover reveals, and excerpts you won't find anywhere else, sign up for her newsletter, or join her over at Historical Hellions, her fan group!

Printed in Great Britain
by Amazon